DOWN SOUTH

ALSO BY WILL ZUBEK:

Narco Gringo
(Tony Winslow series #2)

The characters and events portrayed in this book are fictitious. Any similarity to real persons, living or dead, is coincidental and not intended by the author.

ISBN (paperback): 978-1-7356236-4-1
ISBN (e-book): 978-1-7356236-5-8

Book design by Will Zubek.
Cover design by Alejandro Baigorri.

FIRST EDITION published by Lucky Jake Press.

1 3 5 7 9 0 8 6 4 2

WILL ZUBEK

DOWN SOUTH

ONE

I moved down here just a few weeks after turning forty, and I chose Oaxaca, in part, because no one stateside could pronounce it properly. Whenever I was back home over the holidays, just saying the name of the place—*Wah-haw-kuh*—made clear the divide that existed between us, me and my friends in Chicago, these functioning adults with kids, mortgages, responsibilities. I lived in a small casita about a block from the beach, six hundred square feet or so. It didn't have A/C—not even a window unit—but I did have four fans strategically located throughout the place, aimed directly at the spots I frequented most often: couch, bed, kitchen, toilet (I didn't have IBS or anything, but I did suffer from the occasional bout of food poisoning, and if you think the beef chimichangas at your local Tex-Mex joint do you in from time to time, try experiencing the real thing down here—*then* you'd understand the fan placement).

Another reason I decided to relocate: I could live comfortably in Oaxaca for just a fraction of what it took up in the States. I also spoke fairly decent Spanish, and it was this quasi-bilingualism that had endeared me to a few local families—kind, generous people who invited me into their lives like I was some long-lost cousin (or, more likely, a weird uncle). I went to weddings, birthday parties, quinceañeras. Anything involving lots of food and alcohol, I was there, and usually in a seersucker suit with white linens, the walking embodiment of "Down South" by Tom Petty. If I wore this up in the States I'd look like a walking mid-life crisis. But as an expat in Mexico, it worked. (I think; I hope.) Whenever I pulled out the suit, I knew I was about to have a great time, and by that I mean: eat to the point of discomfort, get blackout drunk, and absolutely hate myself for two days afterwards.

It had been like this for a little over four years: undeserved smooth sailing for a privileged white American expat. But then came the night of Laura Reyes' quinceañera, a huge party her family threw for her fifteenth birthday. (*Quinceañeras* are kind of like sweet sixteens up in the States, only bigger and actually somewhat enjoyable.) I'd become friends with her dad over the years, thanks largely to my habit of buying fruit and vegetables out of the bed of his truck once a week (this was me trying—in vain—to counteract all the chorizo and booze I was consuming).

It was a little after 3:00 a.m. when I started stumbling home from the Reyes farm, which was only about a mile outside of town. Though walking alone in the middle of the night wasn't a great idea, I'd made this same journey many times before, and more often than not I did so while highly inebriated. Besides, I considered Punta Cita my home at this point. I was comfortable there. I knew how to keep myself safe. I knew when and where I might run into trouble, and also when and where I wouldn't. The walk back from Carlos's place: no problem.

I'd just spotted lights from Calle Dorado up ahead—the main road through town, a hundred feet away—when I heard some noise coming from my left: this soft, muffled sort of... *groaning?* I stopped walking, tried listening more closely.

Nothing.

Maybe it was just some animals scurrying around?

Or was I so fucked up that I was imagining things?

Maybe.

Probably.

I started walking again, but then there it was: that same noise. I knew *where* it was coming from—up ahead, to the left, just off the dirt road—but still didn't know *what* it was.

I stopped. Listened some more.

Words in English: *Shut the fuck up.*

Then another voice: *Por favor, no…*

No thinking, just moving: I rushed towards the voices—stumbling around trees, plowing through bushes—until I arrived at a small clearing. Even through the darkness, I could see the outline of two figures on the ground, about twenty feet in front of me. I couldn't fully make out shapes or body parts, but it was obvious what was happening.

I ran towards the figures and lowered my shoulder like I'd been some all-state middle linebacker in high school (the reality: I was a third-string safety who only ever saw the field during blowouts, and even then it was just on special teams). The result: helmet to helmet, fifteen-yard unsportsmanlike. Things went a little blurry after that, but I didn't lose consciousness. Not yet.

After falling to the ground and blindly rolling around for a moment, I reached out and grabbed this other person—this man—by the shirt. I somehow then managed to get up on my knees and start throwing punches. I didn't connect on the first few, but I did land a couple—first his chest, then his face. Most importantly, the clumsy melee gave the woman who'd been underneath the guy an opportunity to get up and run away. As the sound of her footsteps faded, I continued throwing punches. Things were going fairly well until my adrenaline faded and drunken exhaustion took over, at which point my combatant managed to work himself free from my grip. He stood up and tried to run but tripped over the shorts at his ankles. Take two was more successful.

I stayed on the ground for a long while after he ran away, just lying there, staring up at the sky. Heavy panting eventually relaxed into my normal, generally out-of-shape breathing. I didn't know this at the time, of course, but not all those stars I was seeing were up in the sky.

☼

When I woke up the next morning, the amount of pressure in my head made me think I'd just set a new personal record for hangover misery (especially for a night that hadn't involved anything harder than booze and pot). But then I remembered I wasn't just dealing with a normal hangover: there was also the head-to-head contact from just a few hours earlier. I laid there for a long time then, staring up at a sky so blue—so cloudless, so goddamn perfect—that it almost seemed to be mocking me. I didn't dare move my head. Was it even *possible* for me to move my head? Hell, maybe that was the best strategy: just never move again. For a while this actually seemed like a practical approach, but then the thirst and overall misery became too much. I moved my head slightly, a little test drive of sorts, and dear Christ it felt awful, much worse than I'd anticipated. I wasn't just *feeling* the pulsing in my head—I was also hearing it. But I kept at it, kept moving, because I knew if I didn't, I'd probably die right there out of some combination of exposure, dehydration, and apathy. I rolled over, got to my knees, and stood up. Balance precarious, I plodded over to the road then walked about hundred feet out to Calle Dorado.

The first person I saw was Javy Rodriguez. Like me, Javy had been at Laura Reyes' quinceañera. Unlike me, however, he didn't look like a walking human corpse. He'd indulged himself nearly as much as I had, but there was a key difference here: he was about twenty years younger than me. Never before had our age gap been so apparent.

He walked towards me with an impossibly small shortboard under his arm. Javy was the best surfer in Punta Cita—it wasn't even close, really—and he could even hold his own down in Puerto Escondido during a big swell, when a bunch of pros would fly in and act like they owned the place. "*No te vi esta mañana*. Waves were good."

"Had a little too much fun last night."

"Yeah, you look like shit."

"I feel like shit."

He laughed, slapped my shoulder, and ran off.

Back at my casita, I peeled off my seersucker suit and formerly white linens. I hadn't realized how filthy and mangled they were, but now at least all those concerned looks I received on the way home made more sense. I hopped in the shower and stayed there for a half-hour. It helped, but not as much as I'd hoped. I was in a fog. I crawled into bed without drying off, then passed out about two seconds after my head hit the pillow.

☼

I woke up a few hours later, feeling better but also still pretty fucking terrible. I rolled out of bed and walked to La Hija's, figuring a little hair of the dog might do me some good. It did, which resulted in me having even more hair of the dog as I sat at the bar and chatted with the owner, Carlita, about a number of things, including why I looked like I shit. I mentioned the quinceañera but not the walk home. I was hoping the booze would get me in a better headspace, and maybe then I'd be able to remember more than just the highlights: man, woman, fight, blackout. Then I could go to the police and offer up something useful, incompetent and corrupt as though they might be in southern Mexico (not that this is much different from elsewhere in the world, including the U.S.).

A couple hours into my pseudo rehab session, I heard a few loud phrases in English coming from my left, from out on Calle Dorado. This wasn't abnormal. Like most bars in Punta Cita, La Hija's was a mix of locals, expats, and tourists. I looked over and saw three guys in their early 20's walking into the bar. Typical surfer bros, the kind that traveled in packs and usually had at least one trust funder among the crew. One member of the group stood out: he had a square, abnormally large face and bright yellow hair that went down to his shoulders. And though he was relatively tall, maybe 6′2″, he had a blocky physique, the kind you get when you spend way too much time in a gym.

As he got closer, I noticed something else about him: he had a few cuts and bruises on his face. I looked down at my right hand, at the cuts on my knuckles. I'd been too focused on drinking away my post-concussion symptoms to have noticed them earlier.

The group sat down at a table behind me. I listened as they ordered three Pacíficos and a basket of patacones. I tried eavesdropping but couldn't pick up much beyond their drink and food orders. Their general vibe, however, came through loud and clear: loud, annoying, and entitled.

I was asking Carlita for another beer—my third "last one"—when I heard it: *Shut the fuck up!* And then some more laughter. If there'd been any doubt before, there wasn't anymore. Pressure building in my chest, I walked to the bathroom and splashed water on my face. *What the hell do I do now?* I stared at my reflection in the mirror, jumbled mess of thoughts racing through my mind. When I walked back out to the bar, I grabbed a stool closer to the trio's table. Carlita gave me a look but didn't ask any questions. Most likely she just assumed I was already drunk and that I'd forgotten where I was sitting.

I could hear better from my new spot, including this tidbit: they'd be in town for another few days, unfazed as they were, apparently, about the possibility of facing legal repercussions for sexual assault. I wondered if the leader had even told his two underlings what happened. I stood up and started towards the door. I'd head to the police station, file a report (or whatever the hell I'd have to do), walk back to La Hija's, and point at the yellow-haired mutant: *Arrest that evil, weird-looking fucker.*

A wave of a nausea came over me as soon as I stepped onto Calle Dorado, so I figured a quick stop at my place would probably be a good idea. I was looking down and fumbling with my keys as I rounded the corner of my place, so I didn't see the two women standing by the front gate until I'd practically run into them. One was Marysol, a short, middle-aged woman you could usually find running a fruit stand at a little plaza in town. The other was her daughter, Paloma, who was usually right there with her, cutting pineapples and mangos for red-faced tourists.

It was the look in their eyes. I knew right away.

TWO

Kitchen table, three glasses of water.

Marysol, staring down at her hands: *"La culpa es mia."*

They'd had a good night, one of their best ever. After closing up the fruit stand, Marysol gave Paloma a little bit of cash and told her to go have some fun with her friend, Luisa. This wasn't just a rare indulgence for the women from Guatemala—it was the first of its kind. (The three of them had arrived together in Mexico just a couple years prior. They'd considered going all the way north to the U.S. but figured it would be too dangerous, both the journey and the destination.) Paloma and Luisa ended up going to Froggie's, the closest thing to a dance club in Punta Cita. They hadn't even made it through their first beer when three gringos walked over and started trying out their Spanish: *¿Cómo estás? ¿Otra cerveza?* Even though ignorant, entitled assholes weren't their type, the two girls responded *Bien, gracias* and *Sí, gracias* and had themselves another round. Though they didn't understand much of the conversation that ensued, they laughed whenever the guys did, who seemed to enjoy that quite a bit. Mostly, however, they just drank their beers and stole glances at one another: *Is suffering through this worth the free drinks?*

"The guys were really drunk," Marysol continued, telling me the story so her daughter didn't have to. *"Muy, muy borrachos."*

The girls got up after just the one free beer, saying *Gracias, pero lo siento.* They couldn't stay out any longer, they had to work tomorrow. One of the guys—the tall one with yellow hair—jumped up and blocked their way, saying, *"¿Más cerveza? ¿Más cerveza?"*

"Lo siento, no podemos."

After a few more failed attempts to get the girls to stick around, the ringleader eventually moved aside. Paloma and Luisa left the place and walked along Calle Dorado for a while, past all the bars and restaurants. Night over, heading home, laughing about the idiots they'd just encountered.

Until they heard a man's voice, coming from somewhere behind them: *Hey!*

They turned around to find the three guys from Froggie's walking towards them. I wondered if they knew right away, if their hearts stopped and stomachs sank. Did they grab each other's hand? Did they look down at the ground for a rock, for something that might be able to do a little damage?

One of the guys said something in English that included "hotel" and "party," but the women just repeated their line from earlier: *No podemos*. They smiled, trying to hide their nervousness (God forbid you spurn an entitled gringo). Then they turned around and started walking again.

But they didn't get far. The ringleader grabbed Paloma's arm, twisting her around. She shook herself free and even managed to force out some contrived laughter, like they were all just kidding around. *Ha-ha! Jokes! Jokes!*

The blonde-haired mutant grabbed her arm again, much harder this time. When Paloma spun back around to face him, she used her free hand to slap his face. It didn't do much damage, but it did allow her wiggle free from his grip. She tried running, but it was hopeless. While this battle was being waged—Square Face vs. Paloma—the ringleader's two underlings had each grabbed one of Luisa's arms. One of them had also put a hand over her mouth.

It was a little while later that I stumbled across Paloma getting assaulted.

"What happened with Luisa?" I asked.

Marysol shook her head. Paloma kept staring at the table.

"Jesus Christ..." It wasn't just the leader of the pack who was evil: his two sidekicks were, too. They weren't just enablers. They were willing, active participants. An overwhelming sense of shame came over me: if I hadn't been so drunk—if I wasn't such a fucking degenerate—I might have been able to help Luisa, too.

A moment later, Marysol looked up at me and said, "*Gracias. Muchísimas gracias.*"

"For what?"

"*Por la ayuda,*" she said, reaching over and touching her daughter's forearm.

"*Gracias, señor,*" said Paloma, though her eyes remained fixated on the table.

"Please," I said, "just call me Tony." Immediately after saying this I felt like smashing my head off the table. *I know you were sexually assaulted last night, but hey—at least now you know that I'm chill, that you can call me by my first name!*

Marysol then started thanking God for His timing, for putting me on *that* road on *that* night at *that* very moment. My interpretation of the events was a bit different, but I wasn't so clueless that I would start questioning her coping mechanism. So I didn't ask her why God would allow such a heinous act to happen in the first place, or why *He* didn't think Luisa was worthy of having *her* sexual assault get interrupted.

But I did ask this: "Do you want me to go to the police with you?"

For the first time all night, Paloma's eyes darted away from the table, up towards her mom.

"No vamos a la policía," said Marysol.

"¿Qué?"

"No vamos a la policía."

"What? You *have* to go—"

"We *can't* go to the police," she said, with a tone indicating that her decision here was final. "We're from Guatemala," she added, as if that was all the explanation that was needed. "They'd just deport us. We can't."

I wanted to tell her that she was wrong, that there was no way the police would focus on their immigration status instead of the sexual assaults that had taken place. But I wasn't 100% certain on this. Just like any country on earth, Mexico has its fair share of anti-immigrant animosity. It's stupid and illogical and depressing—but it exists, it's real. As an American expat, I was accustomed to being well-protected. I knew that if anything ever happened, I had a U.S. passport and a little bit of money: one was sufficient, and two made me practically invincible. Marysol, Paloma, and Luisa had neither, so they had good reason to be worried. There was a chance the higher-ups in Oaxaca would be more worried about what might happen to their tourism industry if they put three Americans in jail for something the gringos would undoubtedly deny—as opposed to, you know, seeking truth and justice in the sexual assault cases.

Breaking news: the world is fucked.

But I wasn't ready to give up. "I can pay for a lawyer, help you get in contact with the embassy.

Whatever you want. Seriously, we have to do *something.*"

Marysol acted like she hadn't heard a word I just said. She reached for my hand and placed a rosary into my palm. "*Gracias por todo.*"

A minute later I was walking them to the front door, then watching as they disappeared into the night. These two women had been through more shit than I could ever begin to comprehend. They were better people: kinder, braver, stronger. More deserving. Yet here they were, held hostage by two things they had no control over: where they were born and imaginary lines drawn on a map.

There was a protruding nail in the kitchen I'd been meaning to take out for years, ever since I'd moved in. But I never did, due to some combination of laziness and apathy. I walked over and hung up the rosary. I wasn't religious but figured what the hell, what could it hurt?

☼

I spent the rest of the night sitting out on my back patio, drinking beer and wondering what I should do next, if anything. If the women didn't want to go to police, what options did I have?

"God damn everything…" I said, probably several times.

There was a small shed in my backyard, a Craftsman-style thing that looked like it was straight out of a 1995 Sears catalog. It didn't match the style of the casita (white stucco walls, red tile roof), but things in Punta Cita are more about functionality than aesthetics. Waves breaking just a hundred yards away, I considered the boards in the shed: one for every swell, every condition. I'd already missed one good day and didn't want to miss another, so I finished off the beer in my hand, smoked a bowl (sleep would have been impossible otherwise), and climbed into bed. It took some time, even being stoned, but eventually I drifted off to sleep.

☼

My arms felt like jelly paddling out the next morning. I'd just about made it through the impact zone (the area where waves curl and break on your head) when I saw Javy spin around, take a couple of effortless strokes, and drop into a shoulder-high wave. I duck dived and popped out on the other side, but I was still too far inside to go for the next wave, so I paddled up and over it. But the third wave of the set: I had a chance.

Well: *maybe* had a chance.

I didn't think much about what I did next, which is a good thing, generally speaking: the less thinking you do while surfing, the better. I sat up, spun my board around, and then leaned forward and started paddling towards shore. Water rising up beneath me, I paddled *hard,* shoulders screaming at me each time I dug into the water.

Paddle, paddle—

Go, go, fucking go—

One more stroke, one more—

Go, go, go—

I pushed up on the board and slid my feet underneath me, crouching low, left foot out front, looking down the face of the wave. I touched the wall of water with my right hand, fingers grazing glassy blue.

For the next few seconds, I was gone.

Completely, totally *gone.*

Despite my innate ability to overthink and ruin any even potentially enjoyable moment in life, this curse was no match for riding a wave: it's pure bliss, a fleeting sort of nothingness. Only problem is that all waves do eventually come to an end.

"*Buena ola, tío!*" Javy called out.

"You too," I said, paddling towards him.

"I should've waited."

Javy's only real shortcoming was his overeagerness: he went for everything, and oftentimes he'd end up on the first wave of a set, which are typically the smallest. But this was just a natural extension of how he lived his life: enjoying everything as much as possible—right here, right now. His personality was infectious, and you couldn't help but like the guy, even though deep down you kind of wanted to hate to him. He was a little over six-foot tall, had about 1% body fat, and shared a striking physical resemblance with Gabriel Medina, the Brazilian world surfing champ.

"How long you been out?" I asked.

"About an hour," he said, which meant that it must have still been dark when he paddled out. "I've got a bunch of lessons later today."

"First timers?"

"This morning, yeah."

"Fun."

He laughed. "Yeah, dude. A blast. There's also this group from yesterday I have to go out with again. Three assholes from the States, got a week's worth of lessons. Maybe my least favorite group I've ever had."

"Three guys?"

"Yeah. First time out the other day, yet they're blaming the waves, the boards, the wind. Guys haven't even surfed before! And it was a *good* day, dude. Waves were perfect, even in the afternoon."

"Javy, these guys..." I said, but he wasn't listening—he was spinning around and going for the first wave of the next set. The rule about talking in the lineup is that it doesn't matter what's being discussed, doesn't matter how serious—your wife just filed for divorce; your mom just died; your failed suicide attempt from the night before, and how you're thinking about trying again right now, this very moment—once a set starts rolling in, the other person is under no obligation to stick around and hear you finish your thought.

Whatever calmness (or peace, tranquility, whatever) I'd managed to obtain after my first wave was now gone. The rest of the set passed beneath me as I bobbed in the water, staring out at the horizon, debating whether I should tell Javy about everything that happened these past few days. The advantages of telling him: he'd offer some perspective, which would probably help me walk back from the ledge, even just a little bit. He'd talk me out of my worst ideas. The disadvantages: I'd be getting him involved in something that wasn't his problem. Even though I'd never really seen him get too worked up about anything, I wasn't sure how he'd react to something like this.

"Those three guys," I said, once he'd paddled back out. "What time's their lesson?"

"This afternoon, I think 3:00."

Another set was already coming in. Beautiful day, perfect swell.

"Why? You know them?"

"No," I said, after a moment. "Just curious."

I turned and paddled for the first wave of the next set. Almost pearled on the goddamn thing. (Pearling: if you're not paddling fast enough, or if you're too late getting into the wave, the back end of your board gets lifted up by the rising water and you head straight down—headfirst—along with the breaking wave. Fun stuff.) I'd pearled on many occasions before, but this time I somehow managed to overcome my slow paddling and bad timing.

I dropped into the wave, and then for a few seconds: *gone.*

But then it was over, and my mind immediately jumped ahead to 3:00 p.m. Could I ask Javy to take the guys out to one of the many secluded surf spots nearby? To this one in particular, where not only was the wave heavy, but there were also rocks sprinkled throughout the impact zone. If the three fuckers messed up there—which they certainly would—they'd be in some serious trouble. Hell, if I was honest with myself about my own abilities—if I was smart, sensible—I wouldn't have ever surfed there myself. (But I did. Often.)

I ended up not saying anything, and Javy and I simply traded waves for another hour, until a few other people paddled out and joined the lineup. Most were tourists, including a young couple from Germany with zinc oxide all over their faces and bucket hats on their heads. I don't believe they caught a single wave.

For a few fleeting moments on each wave, I was good—relaxed, carefree, unconcerned. But then the wave would peter out, and my thoughts would immediately jump ahead to later that afternoon.

I had to do something.

And I would.

It was just a matter of what.

☼

After a late-morning nap (no amount of anxiety can match post-surfing fatigue), I walked into town and got breakfast at El Cafecito, where I flipped through a week-old copy of *La Jornada* and stuffed my face with a double serving of huevos rancheros. Though I'd gotten pretty good at ignoring all of the awful political, social, and environmental news from around the world (in other words: I was a terrible, entitled person), it was a different experience to have witnessed something so horrific in person. It was all I could think about. There was no off switch. I couldn't just pretend like it hadn't happened. While I'd accepted plenty of flaws about myself (*I'm self-centered, I'm lazy, I'm…*), turning a blind eye to two women getting sexually assaulted was a bridge too far.

After gaining five pounds in about ten minutes, I put on my twenty-peso aviators and started walking along Calle Dorado, the main drag through town that ran parallel to the beach. A couple minutes later I was walking into La Panadería de Arturo, a bakery whose air alone could turn a person diabetic. Gilberto Jiménez was in the far back corner of the place, sitting directly underneath an overhead fan, empty plate on the table in front of him (best guess, based on the color and position of crumbs: three pastries, different kinds). I ordered coffee at the counter, then walked over and sat down at the small table next to his.

"*¿Cómo va?*"

"*Pues, bueno,*" he said, not taking his eyes off the newspaper he was pretending to read.

"Can I run a hypothetical by you?"

He laughed.

"Like a what-if."

He put the paper down and took a long drink from his liter bottle of Coca-Cola (yes: liter). The highest-ranking state cop in Punta Cita, Gilberto was well-known for looking the other way—or not—depending on the amount of financial contributions from interested parties. He wasn't so powerful that you couldn't ever go against him, but doing that would be akin to winning the battle but losing the war. It might take him some time, but he'd eventually get you back.

"I know what a hypothetical is, Tony."

"I figured, but… anyway, say a person comes across someone getting sexually assaulted…" I ran through it then: basic premise, no names, third-person narrator.

"Could the person who intervened identify the suspect?"

"Probably."

He let out a long exhale. I couldn't tell whether he was annoyed with me or out of breath from just, like, existing.

"And the victims here, who are they?"

"Does it matter?"

"Of course not. Just a question. We don't have a prejudice down here, unlike up in *los Estados Unidos*."

I almost laughed. Sure, the U.S. has a judicial system that's far from perfect—just like every other country on earth inhabited by human beings—but it was irritating to have a cop well-known for being up for sale sit there and lecture me about ethics. But I'd learned early on in Mexico that whenever you're confronted with absurdity or hypocrisy (or some combination of the two), the best approach is to smile, take a deep breath, and then, most importantly, *accept* the bullshit. Otherwise you'd lose your fucking mind.

"I know," I said, even though I knew there'd be a huge difference in how Gilberto would treat poor migrants from Guatemala compared to rich tourists from the States. I could see him *maybe* arresting the three guys (and holding some self-serving press conference?), but the much more likely scenario was that he'd hold out his sausage link fingers and happily accept a bribe worth a few months' salary (which, of course, would be pocket change to the American trust funders). The guys would then fly back to the U.S. and get on with their lives, like nothing at all had happened. Years later they'd get together and laugh about the little pickle they got themselves into down in Mexico. *Thank god for that fat ass cop!*

I also had to worry about what might happen to Marysol, Paloma, and Luisa if they got pressed about their immigration status. Their only reward for reporting the assaults might be getting sent back to Guatemala, a place from which they'd recently fled.

"*¿Eso es todo?*" Gilberto asked.

"That's all," I said, standing up. "Thanks for hearing me out."

As I walked outside, I wondered what I'd accomplished with this little visit.

It didn't take me long to settle on an answer: not a goddamn thing.

☼

I had some time to kill that afternoon, so I wandered away from the beach, heading north on a dirt road until I came to a small gringa-run yoga studio. Kerstin was sitting outside on a small patio, reading a book about herbs native to Oaxaca.

"How many strains of pot does that cover?"

"None."

"Why bother then?"

"Because not all of us can survive on rice and beans without any seasoning."

"I eat eggs. And potatoes."

"That right?"

"And chorizo."

"Anything else?"

I shrugged. "Sometimes."

"I must be getting you confused with someone else I know."

"Someone else? You trying to make me jealous?"

She laughed. "You look familiar, I swear, but I can't… I'm having a hard time placing you."

"Elderly Woman Behind the Counter in a Small Town."

"What?"

"It's a Pearl Jam song. About a woman who can't remember someone's face."

"So that's why I haven't seen you much lately? You're— what— paying homage to Eddie Vedder?"

I couldn't tell from her tone whether this was playful jabbing or some genuine annoyance. "Would that make it better or worse for me?"

"Good question."

Originally from Sweden, Kerstin had followed a path similar to my own: failed relationships and existential crises up until age forty, followed shortly thereafter by eventual acceptance: *I guess I'm just not cut out for this*. For me, "this" meant life in Chicago, and for her, life in Stockholm. So she moved to Mexico, figuring, essentially, *Why not?*

I'd watched many people have a go at expat life: they'd quit their jobs and sell their homes in D.C., Toronto, Munich, and "start a new life" in southern Mexico. But many would only last a year or two—sometimes not even that—before getting on a plane and heading home, or at least to a bigger city in Mexico, one with paved roads and a nearby airport. Kerstin and I, however, had both managed to make it work in Punta Cita, and in that simple fact we'd found something in common. She also had an independent streak that matched my own, so we weren't so much in a relationship as having agreed—without ever stating as much—that our paths could cross from time to time. Sometimes we'd see each other on a daily basis, and other times we'd go weeks without seeing each other at all.

"How's the garden?" I asked.

"Good. I gave you some hoja santa last time, right?"

"You did, yeah," I said, though I couldn't remember what she'd given me, nor whether I'd tried it. For me, herbs fell into two categories: (1) cilantro and (2) everything else.

After chatting for a while about the usual stuff (annoying clients, waves, etc.), her face suddenly took on a serious look: "You okay, Tony?"

This simple question somehow flustered me, and I felt this strong urge to tell her—everything, all of it.

But it was the same now with Kerstin as it had been earlier with Javy: I couldn't put this on someone else.

"All good," I said, though I nearly choked on the two simple words. "Why do you ask?"

"You just seem a little off."

I shrugged. "I'm not sure why."

☼

After buying a couple Pacíficos at a corner tienda, I walked to the beach and sat down on a fallen tree. I then watched as Javy pushed the three young rapists into small, mushy waves. All beginning surfers are terrible, but this crew took it to another level. And their vibes were all off: they were frustrated, impatient, annoyed. They acted as though a couple of lessons should have turned them into Kelly Slater.

Ten minutes later, second beer, I focused in on the square-faced ringleader, his cuts and scrapes hidden underneath a thick swath of zinc oxide. I briefly considered swimming out and trying to strangle him with his leash, but I wasn't sure I'd be able to do so before Javy or one of his buddies could intervene. And then, of course, I'd have to strangle the other two. No way I could manage that.

Feeling some combination of nausea, anger, and helplessness, I decided to abandon this ill-conceived viewing session. I was also out of beer. Walking back to my place, I wondered if they were even remorseful. They should have been haunted by what they'd done, but instead they were out at the bar the very next night, and a day after that they were taking surf lessons.

Fuck them.

Fuck them.

For dinner I opened a can of beans and poured them over some leftover rice I found in the back of the fridge (mold-free; always check first). After subjecting myself to that, I opened up *East of Eden* and flipped around until I found a passage with Lee in it, hoping some of his words of wisdom might be applicable to my current situation. This didn't work, though the fault was my own—not Lee's, not Steinbeck's. I couldn't think straight, let alone read and digest literature. Fortunately, my restlessness was no match for the fatigue brought on by a couple of hours in the sun, a few beers, and a plateful of carbs. My second siesta of the day came on involuntarily.

☼

Later that evening I woke up feeling somewhat refreshed. Such is the beauty of the siesta. I drank a glass of water, grabbed a beer from the fridge, and started walking towards La Hija's. Javy was already at the bar: Corona, no lime. I sat down beside him and slid over my empty can. Carlita was ready with another Pacífico.

"Not much out there this afternoon," he said.

"Huh?"

"I saw you at the beach earlier."

"Oh, yeah," I said. "Cross-shores were too strong."

"Yeah, and too much northwest in the swell."

I took a long pull from my fresh beer. "Those guys looked like quite a crew."

"Who?"

"Those three guys. Americans, I think you said?"

"Fuck, man," he said, shaking his head. "Gets worse every day."

"Yeah?"

"For one, they regularly use the word *mamacita*."

"Jesus Christ."

"And they're just so…"

"Entitled?"

"That's normal for tourists. These guys take it to another level."

"*Mamacitas*?" I said. "Really?"

"Swear to god."

We sat and drank beers until happy hour was about to come to an end. Though Carlita gave us special pricing regardless of the time of day, Javy had a routine: he'd buy one last beer right before happy hour ended, drink it slowly, and then go hang out with any number of women more than happy to have him stop by for an hour or two. After that, he'd put his board shorts back on, walk home, and go to bed earlier than anyone I knew under the age of sixty. (A few of his friends called him "Javiejo," a mash-up of "Javy" and "viejo," the latter of which means "old man" in Spanish. Creative bunch.)

But on this night things were different. Happy hour ended, but Javy kept ordering beers. A little while later came shots of tequila. It was a rare sight, watching him get shitfaced like this, but since it was a Friday night and the surf forecast for tomorrow was shit, I figured that probably explained it. As for me, it was just another day—Friday, Tuesday, Sunday, it didn't matter. The question wasn't so much *Why get drunk?* as *Why not?*

A few hours later, once we were both sufficiently sauced, he leaned over and said, "I'm in some trouble, *hermano. Una mujer.*"

I laughed, assuming I was about to hear yet another tale of unrequited love. This happened from time to time with him: girl takes surf lesson, girl falls in love, girl wants to move to Mexico. These stories typically didn't involve anything too wild—just a few rambling love letters, unhinged voicemails, and missed flights—but every once in a while they'd venture into *Fatal Attraction* territory: girl shows up with a suitcase a week later and says, *Surprise! I'm back, and now I'm moving in!*

"How bad is it?"

Javy stared at the bar, shaking his head. "I… it's… yeah…"

"Holy shit," I laughed. "Have we encountered a new level of crazy?"

He finished off his beer and gestured for Carlita to bring him another. When he looked over at me, he had this weird sort of smile on his face. "I think I'm in love, dude."

I laughed so hard I nearly fell off my barstool (reminder: I was drunk, and also desperate for distraction, humor, anything). Despite my over-the-top reaction, the expression on his face didn't change. He wasn't joking. There was no punchline. Carlita brought him another Corona and asked me what was so goddamn funny.

"Nada," Javy said, answering for me. *"Tony está borracho."*

This might have been true, but so too was Javy. We were both shitfaced. After Carlita walked away, I said, "You're being serious?"

He shrugged.

"Congrats, I guess?"

"It's not that simple."

"Why not?"

"She's married."

"Happily?"

He laughed, shook his head.

"Just a small hurdle, man."

"It's complicated."

"Not *that* complicated. There are legal proceedings for this kind of thing."

I asked for more information—her name, how they met, where she was from, all that stuff—but couldn't get much out of him. As the drinks kept coming and our BACs crept steadily higher, I started thinking that it was *my* turn to tell *him* something personal. I was also incredibly drunk at this point, even by my degenerate standards.

"I need to run something by you."

"*Dime*," he said. *Dee-may*. "Anything."

One benefit of having incessantly replayed everything in my mind the past few days: no level of inebriation could have prevented me from providing a thorough recap of the events. After my not-so-brief monologue, Javy sat there staring at the bar for a long moment. Without saying a word to me, he asked Carlita for two doubles of tequila.

Then, in what was either perfect or terrible timing, the three bros walked in a few minutes later. Each was rocking a different Patagonia t-shirt. *Live Simply, and by that we mean pay $70 for a shirt made of sheep pubes.*

"*Tenemos que hacer algo*," he said, glaring over at them.

"I agree. But what?"

We turned around on our barstools and looked out across a small dance floor. A few people moved to some reggae music, but mostly it was the buzz of the crowd that I heard. Tables surrounded the dance floor: groups of friends, empty beer bottles. Chatter, laughter.

The three bros stood off to the side, figuring out their next move.

"They probably struck out at Froggie's," said Javy.

I watched as the trio walked over to a table with two girls sitting around it. Plopped themselves right down—no introductions, no questions. *Hey, what's up? Anyone in these seats? Mind if we sit here?* It was a small miracle they'd found three empty chairs in the place, but sometimes the universe just fucking sucks like that.

The newly formed group of five then chatted for a few minutes, the girls laughing self-consciously as the crew's ringleader, Square Face, did most of the talking. His two sidekicks seemed content in playing supporting roles, nodding in agreement, adding laughter when appropriate.

"What do you think?" I said, turning to face Javy. "Should we..."

He stood up. "*Vamos.*"

"Huh? What are we—"

But the place was too loud and Javy was already walking. I stood up and followed him across the dance floor.

"*Sal de aquí,*" he said to the two women. "*Estos hombres son pendejos, ¿me entienden?*"

The women looked at Javy, then at each other. Understandably, they both seemed fairly confused.

"*Sal de aquí,*" he said again, with a more forceful tone this time. "*Ahora mismo.*"

This was all it took. Had anyone else tried this stunt, they might have laughed in his face. But not Javy. People listened to Javy. The two women stood up, grabbed their purses, and left without saying a word.

While the trio of rapists had initially seemed stoked to have their surf instructor walk over to their table—no doubt he was about to help them score with some *mamacitas!*—now they were confused and annoyed. And angry.

"What the hell, dude?" said Square Face.

The other two expressed similar sentiments.

Javy sat down in one of the recently vacated chairs. He leaned forward and put his elbows on the table. He gestured for the three of them to do the same.

"You need to leave," he said, his English slow but clear. "Go to the hotel, get some sleep. Then tomorrow you're on the first shuttle. *¿Entendido*? The first one, not the second one, and if I see you again—"

"Javy, what are you talking about?" said Square Face. "We have a lesson with you, with—"

"I know what you did, *hijos de puta*. What all three of you did." He paused so he could take a long look at each one of them. All three looked away, eyes darting to the table, ground, ceiling—anywhere. "Leave. *Ahora mismo*. If I see you again, if I see you at the beach tomorrow—"

"I don't know what you're talking about," muttered Square Face, standing up now, still avoiding eye contact. His two sidekicks were so ready to get out of there that they nearly tripped over themselves.

Javy stood up and blocked their exit route. "You know *exactly* what I'm talking about."

"Dude, you're fucking crazy," said Square Face, though it was clear he had zero interest in seeing how far Javy was willing to take things. He and his two underlings stepped sideways and scurried outside.

Feeling sober all of a sudden, I headed back over to the bar with Javy and ordered another round. I thanked him for what he did, though I also wondered if that had been the right strategy. Kind of felt like all we did was tip them off. *Hey guys, you should go ahead and skip town before you have to face any real repercussions!* But if Marysol, Paloma, and Luisa didn't want to go to the police, what other options did we have?

We drank more, mostly tequila, until a little after 2:00 a.m. (Or was it 3:00 a.m.?) La Hija's was packed, louder than ever. The place was also starting to spin on me.

"Think I'm gonna call it a night," I said.

Javy stood up and gave me a hug. Our balance was precarious but we managed.

"Thanks again," I said, "what you did."

"Wasn't enough."

"I know. It's just, this place is so..."

"Fucked," he said. "This place is *fucked*."

Back at the casita, I lit a half-smoked joint and took a few tokes. Then I forced down a glass of water and a few ibuprofens.

My mind was still racing as I collapsed onto my bed: *That's it? They'll just leave town and get on with their lives?*

I wanted to scream. Maybe I did.

THREE

I woke up the next morning with the distinct sensation that something was pounding against my skull. Some quick math had me thinking I'd need six ibuprofens, three large coffees, and a couple packets of Pedialyte to start feeling normal again.

"Fuck me…" I said, more than once, until finally I realized that the pounding wasn't just in my head—it was also coming from my front door. I rolled out of bed and shuffled to the living room, glancing down briefly to make sure I at least had boxers on (I did). But I didn't bother looking out the window to see who was outside, as that would have required energy and forethought I simply didn't have at this point. After opening the door, the glare from outside immediately added a new dimension to my misery. A wave of nausea didn't so much pass over as crash into me. I bent over at the waist, readying myself for the worst.

Sandals were the first things I saw, then black yoga pants and a faded Smiths t-shirt. These visuals made me feel a little better: Kerstin would be able to brew the coffee, mix the Pedialyte, and, if those didn't work, pour tequila down my throat.

Once I finally managed to get to eye level with her (no puking, just dry heaving), I saw the look on her face and immediately thought, *God damn it, what'd I do?* I couldn't think of anything in particular, which might have been part of the problem. According to a few of my exes (or: all of them), I could be "painfully oblivious" at times. Had I not picked up on her unhappiness? Had our relationship—or whatever the hell it was—become *too* casual? This was my first and only relationship (using this word loosely) in my four years in Mexico. It wasn't anything serious, but it *was* fairly consistent—and mostly, I think, monogamous. Maybe she was craving some more "emotional availability" from me, which was another phrase I'd heard a few times before. (Please note that I'm not proud of these character traits.)

A sinking feeling came over me. Combined with the pounding in my skull and lingering nausea, it was quite the emotional cocktail to start the day.

She walked past me, into the living room. Sat down on the couch without saying a word.

"You want a drink?" I asked. "I have some tea, that stuff you brought over."

These words didn't seem to register with her. She leaned forward, elbows on her knees, staring down at the ground.

Dear god. Could it really be *that* bad?

I sat down beside her, feeling terrible for a variety of reasons. I put a hand on her back, saying, "It's okay. I know I'm not great at these things. I don't do the things I should, or say the right things. But—"

"Tony, no…" she said, shaking her head. "I'm not here because of anything…"

"With us?"

"Yeah— I mean, no. It's not, it's…"

I felt relieved for a brief moment, but then confusion set in: "What is it then? What's wrong?"

"It's Javy…"

Despite a barely functioning brain, I connected the dots right away (or: I thought I did). It felt like getting punched in the stomach. As far as I knew, Javy never crossed the line and fucked around with any of his friends' wives or girlfriends (though he did fuck around with plenty of *non-friends'* wives and girlfriends). Maybe he thought my relationship with Kerstin was too casual to count? Maybe he was right. And as for Kerstin, I didn't think she'd do something like that, sleep with one of my best friends, but—

"Javy died."

Two words. They couldn't have been any simpler, yet my initial reaction was complete incomprehension. I was still drunk. I was high. I was hallucinating. I was—

"Last night."

I shook my head. "I saw him last night. I was with him."

"Tony..."

I understood now: she was using the wrong words. She'd gotten confused, mixed up her vocabulary. I had to remember: English wasn't her first language.

"I saw him," I said again, shaking my head. "Last night. I was with him."

She turned and grabbed both of my hands. "I'm so sorry, Tony. He's— Javy's dead."

Suddenly it felt like I was sucking air through a straw. "How can— are you sure?"

She nodded.

"How?"

"I don't know. They found his body this morning."

I thought back to the night before. Things were fuzzy but I could remember the highlights.

La Hija's.

Beer.

Tequila.

Lots of it.

Too much.

A conversation with three guys.

I got up from the couch and rushed to the bathroom. I kneeled down by the toilet and emptied my stomach. Then I sat down on the floor and leaned back against the wall. My head was on fire—and also my stomach, my chest. Everything.

Kerstin came in a little while later and sat down next to me.

I didn't think then about what I could do, or what I should do. I thought about what I had to do.

☼

A few minutes later I stood up and went over to the sink. Rinsed my mouth out, splashed water on my face.

Kerstin came over and put a hand on my back. "You okay?"

"I'm gonna head into town for a little bit," I said, reaching for a towel.

"Where?"

"Just La Hija's."

"You sure that's a good idea?"

I didn't answer that.

She walked with me until we got to Avenida Azul. "If you want," she said, "I'll go with you."

"It's okay," I said, leaning in, kissing her forehead.

"You sure?"

I smiled. "I'll be fine."

Carlita was a mess—but she was there, behind the bar. We hugged, cried, sobbed. One minute, five minutes, I can't be sure. Eventually I asked, "*¿Qué pasó?*"

She looked up at me, face twisted with grief. "I don't know."

"Do you remember anything? Did you see anything?"

"He left a little after you. He was really drunk, but that's— I mean— I don't know…"

A group of tourists walked into the place a moment later, big smiles on their faces until they looked behind the bar and saw two people having some casual mid-morning breakdowns.

☼

Punta Cita's lone police station was strategically located at the far end of town, placed there so it was the first thing tourists would see when they walked over from the neighboring resort area. (Gotta make the gringos feel safe; otherwise they won't venture out and stimulate the local economy.)

I walked into the station, took off my sunglasses, and looked around. It wasn't a big place, so there wasn't much to see (a few chairs, a desk, a Mexican flag). The young woman at the front desk looked up and considered me for a brief moment, but then her eyes went back down to her phone. She didn't say a word as I walked past her.

Gilberto's office was a pigsty, as I should have expected. Whole place was covered in folders, papers, empty bags of chips, soda bottles.

"Tony Winslow," he said, leaning back in his chair, hands resting on his enormous stomach. He was the kind of guy who almost seemed to take pride in his obesity, like he was some nobleman in the Middle Ages, back when being a fat ass was a sign you were living the good life.

"¿Qué pasó?"

"We won't know for sure until we get the autopsy back."

"What do you *think* happened?"

He pulled out a pack of cigarettes, lit one, and took a long drag. Then, finally: "Hard to say, really."

"Jesus Christ," I said, already losing my patience. "How about you at least *pretend* to give a shit here? Actually do your fucking job?"

"*El gringo héroe,* here to save the day."

"Fuck off."

"It was a head injury."

"What kind?"

"*Contusión.*"

"From what?"

"Hopefully that's what the autopsy will help us figure out."

"But it almost has to mean someone hit him, right?"

"Not necessarily. He could've just been drunk. Fell down, hit his head."

"There's no way—"

"Walking around here in the middle of the night, pitch black." He shook his head. "That's dangerous for a variety of reasons."

I was standing just inside the doorway to his office, in part because there wasn't room anywhere else. I also feared that if I got any closer to Gilberto, I might try to strangle him.

"Listen," I said. "Remember that hypothetical I asked you about? The sexual assault?"

He laughed. "Sure, yeah. The hypothetical."

"What if it wasn't?"

He made a big show of feigning surprise. "No way!"

"So?"

He made a gesture with his hand, like he was a king and I was the jester. *Get on with it, peasant…*

And so I proceeded to dance. Still leaving out the victims' names, I told him about the sexual assault I'd interrupted, and also about the one I hadn't. Then I told him about last night, how Javy told the three guys—the three *rapists*—to get out of Punta Cita. After I was finished, Gilberto stubbed out his cigarette in an ashtray I couldn't see.

"So," he said, "you think they might've hung around and waited for Javy to leave the bar?"

"That's my guess."

"Do you know where they're staying?"

"La Vista del Mar."

Gilberto leaned forward, put his hands on the desk, and hoisted himself up from his chair. This seemed to require a considerable amount of effort. "I'll look into it."

"Want me to go with you?"

He looked at me for a moment. "No, Tony, I do not want you to go with me. The hell you think this is?"

"I'm just—"

"Bring the gringo to work day?"

"Good one. Listen—"

"You listen: I don't want you doing anything at all. I want you to go home and relax, *¿me entiendes?*"

☼

The hardest part about following Gilberto was walking slow enough so that I wouldn't catch up to him. Based on the thousands of episodes of *Law & Order* I'd seen in my life, I knew that the ideal distance to keep between us was about three-quarters of a block. A few times I just had to stop and stand still for a little while, let him get out ahead of me some more. After watching him walk into La Vista del Mar, I headed into the nearest corner store and bought a Pacífico. Ten minutes later I bought another. I was almost through this second beer when Gilberto came walking out of the resort. His eyes immediately landed on me.

"God damn it..." I thought I was far enough away—and hidden well enough—that he wouldn't have been able to spot me. Apparently not. He shook his head and started walking towards me, his pace somehow even slower now.

"You following me, Tony?"

"No," I said, getting in step beside him. "Small town."

He grunted.

"Did you talk to them?"

"I did. And I also spoke to their lawyer on the phone—"

"Their lawyer?"

"Also happens to be the father of two of the guys."

Of course their dad was a lawyer. The other guy's dad was probably... what? A plastic surgeon? Real estate developer?

"They say anything?"

"Just that they'll be on the four o'clock shuttle back to Puerto."

"You're letting them leave?"

"I'm not *letting* them do anything."

I stepped in front of him, blocking his way. "These guys *raped* two women, and then they fucking *killed* somebody. *¿Me entiendes?*"

He took out a handkerchief, wiped his face. "No sexual assaults have been reported, and there's no evidence that they were involved in Javy's death. I can only work with what I have."

"What about everything I just told you?"

"You think one person's guesswork is enough to keep three Americans from leaving the country?"

It felt like my head was about to explode. "Since when does that matter?"

"Since when does what matter?"

"Rules, laws, all that shit."

"The fuck are you talking about, Tony?"

"*¿Cuanto?* How much do you want? That's how this works, right?"

He stared at me for a long moment, beads of sweat rolling down his face.

"I know how this works," I said. "It ain't no secret."

"*Chinga tu madre,*" he said, moving past me, and it was at this moment that something important dawned on me: this *probably* wasn't the best approach. Offering a bribe is one thing, but talking shit and accusing him of being up for sale might have been a *bit* too much. Instead of following him and offering an apology, I headed back into the corner store and bought a couple more Pacíficos. Then I walked to the lone plaza in town. There's a statue of some guy in the middle of the square, though I couldn't ever remember his name or what he'd done to deserve it (my assumptions: rape and pillage). I sat on a bench and looked across the square at Marysol and Paloma, hard at work at the fruit stand: peeling mangos, chopping pineapples, squeezing oranges. Fortunately, they were too busy to notice the gringo staring over at them as he polished off his third and fourth beers of the morning.

I was rudderless. Useless.

I had no ideas.

Fucking *nada*.

But then something happened—or maybe it was just as simple as the alcohol having finally kicked in—and some ideas *did* start coming, one in which involved me heading back over to La Vista del Mar and paying the three bros a visit myself.

I laughed, shaking my head. As if I had the guts. I purchased beers number five and six on the walk back to my place, making a point to not look at the clock behind the register. That way I wouldn't know whether it was before or after noon. Four beers before *mediodía* was a nice little wake-me-up, but five meant there was a problem. (After noon: anything goes.)

"Pues, tienes sed esta mañana," said the old man working the register, small grin on his face. I'd mistakenly assumed he'd be non-judgmental, but now here he was telling me how thirsty I was this morning.

"Hace calor."

"It's always hot," he said. *"Bienvenidos a México."*

I walked along Calle Dorado until I came to Avenida Azul, where I turned right and headed north, away from the beach. A few minutes later I was at Vicente's, an outdoor bar that looked like the kind of pavilion you'd find next to a Little League baseball field up in the States. But instead of picnic tables and rusted grills spread out on the concrete slab, on this one you'd find white plastic chairs and folding tables, along with ten wooden stools lined up in front of a bar. Menu options include three types of beer and two types of tequila. I was a regular visitor for two reasons: the beer was cheap, even by Punta Cita standards, and tourists almost never trekked out to the place.

Sitting at the bar was forty-five-year-old Mateo Sandoval, a man whose age I knew only because I bought him a couple birthday rounds a few weeks earlier. The guy looked eerily similar to El Chapo—short, stout, thick black mustache—and you could find him at Vicente's periodically throughout the day, during his breaks from work. What kind of job allowed him to take frequent booze breaks? He was a driver. Of people. (Remember: Mexico.) More specifically, he was the shuttle bus driver for La Vista del Mar, and he was able to get away with the boozing because he only ever nursed a couple beers between his twice-daily trips. So his BAC never got too high, and like many Mexican men, he regularly doused himself with Drakkar Noir and Axe body spray, which made it highly unlikely—if not impossible—that anyone would ever be able to smell the alcohol on him. Besides, as he liked to theorize, having a little booze in his system actually led to a smoother and safer ride for his passengers. And it really wasn't that bad of an argument: the looseness allowed him to avoid potholes in the road more effectively than the jerky, overcompensating manner of a sober drive. Having made the trip to Puerto Escondido with him on a few occasions, I could offer firsthand testimony in support of the practice. If no one was at the airport in Puerto Escondido waiting to be taken to the resort in Punta Cita (La Vista del Mar offered "free" airport transportation), we'd stick around for a couple hours, drinking beers and eating hamburgers at a greasy "American restaurant" Mateo thought was the best dining establishment in all of Mexico.

I took a seat next to him. *"Mateo, ¿cómo va?"*

"Oye, hombre, ¿qué pasa?"

Vicente brought me a Pacífico without asking. The old guy didn't do anything but smoke and drink all day, yet somehow it looked like he had the body of a triathlete.

After thanking him, I turned to Mateo and said, "I might need a favor."

"*Dime.*" Dee-may. *Tell me.*

I started at the beginning, then told him my plan.

He didn't hesitate—not for one second. Just raised his Tecate, and we clanked cans.

FOUR

Back to my place then, to grab a few things. Didn't take long. I was locking the front door when I heard a familiar voice behind me: "Hey."

I turned around. "Oh, hey," I said, trying to seem as relaxed as possible. "What's up?"

"How you doing?"

"I'm— well, you know— yeah, I'm doing better. How about you?"

"I'm doing all right," Kerstin said, before walking towards me and wrapping her arms around me. I hugged her back but pulled away before her hands could explore the lower part of my back.

"Did you talk with Gilberto?" she asked.

"I did, yeah."

"And?"

"He didn't really offer much."

"Do they think Javy was killed?"

"They have to wait on the autopsy, but…"

"What?"

"I think it's a possibility."

"You think that, or Gilberto thinks that?"

"Given that it was a head injury, I don't know… I can't imagine him just falling and hitting his head, no matter how drunk he was."

She looked at me for a moment before saying, "Why do I feel like you're not telling me something?"

I could have told her right then. Easy. *Fácil.* Open mouth, say words, tell truth. But I didn't. Whether it was because I didn't want to get her involved (for her own sake) or because I didn't want to give her a chance to talk me out of what I was about to do, I don't know.

"Why would you think that?"

"I don't need protected," she said, a bite to her voice that hadn't been there before.

"I'm not— I'm not hiding anything or trying to protect you. I just have a gut feeling, that's all."

"Based on what?"

I'd never been a great liar. "I don't know," I said, struggling to find any meaningful words. "Just— I mean, he was such a good athlete. You've seen him surf, right? He can ride a twenty-foot wave but trips over a rock? It just doesn't add up."

She looked at me for a moment before saying, "Where are you going right now?"

"Just for a walk," I said. "Try to clear my head."

She didn't offer to go with me. For this I was grateful.

It was a Saturday afternoon, so Calle Dorado was full of tourists walking around, stuffing their faces, getting drunk (and locals working hard so they could get drunk later on). A few expats were also scattered about, with members of this tribe typically falling into one of two camps: one, they'd gotten into some trouble with the IRS or DEA, or maybe with some sixteen-year-old girl named Caitlyn in their high school geometry class, so living in Mexico wasn't so much a choice as it was an escape plan; two, they wanted an early retirement but hadn't worked on Wall Street, so breaking free from the nine-to-five required a move to Mexico, where the exchange rate and cost of living allowed them to jump a few social classes.

I made my way through town, past the police station, over into the resort area. Mateo was standing out front of La Vista del Mar, chatting with a groundskeeper. I walked through the resort's gates, veered left, and headed towards the back of the hotel. The van was unlocked, just like he said it'd be. I opened the back door, unfolded the blanket that was inside, and climbed in underneath it. After what felt like an hour but was probably just a few minutes, I heard a door open at the front of the van.

"¿Listo?"

"Sí."

Mateo put the van in drive and pulled around to the front of the resort (I couldn't see any of this, of course, but that was the plan). A minute later I heard him open the door and get out, and then a few seconds after that a side door was opened. Three pairs of feet climbed aboard. In broken English, Mateo told them to put their bags on the seats beside them. It was just the three of them on this trip to Puerto, so there was plenty of space. No need to use the back.

☼

"Man, fuck this place."

I hated the sound of his voice. Fucking *hated* it. Also hated that I knew the sound of it. I was hoping I'd overhear something more substantive (dream scenario: a confession), but those four words were pretty much the extent of their conversation.

A half-hour later I felt the van slowing down. *"Lo siento,"* said Mateo. "Flat tire."

Flat tire. I'd taught him these words just a couple of hours ago at Vicente's, and he'd practiced them until they became the two words of English he could pronounce better than any others. *Hello. Please. Thank you. Flat tire.*

"Are you fucking kidding me?" said Square Face, after Mateo hopped out and shut the door.

I heard feet crunching on gravel, the back door opening up. Mateo then lifted the blanket off of me, and if I had any lingering doubts about going through with this, the look in his eyes rid me of those.

The three other guys in the van didn't know this, but Mateo had veered off the main road to Puerto Escondido shortly after leaving the resort. He'd then taken several turns on winding backroads before stopping along the outskirts of land owned by Carlos Reyes, the farmer who'd thrown the *quinceañera* for his daughter just a few days earlier.

Quietly as I could manage, I sat up and crawled out of the van, then ducked low and ran into the dense forest beside the road. I positioned myself behind a tree as Mateo walked around the side of the van, opened a door, and asked for some help with the flat tire. Square Face muttered a few things under his breath as he walked around to the back of the van, though I couldn't make out what. The other two didn't seem too amused either.

Once their backs were turned, I stepped out from the behind the tree and started moving. My legs: straight fucking *jelly*. Felt like I was floating. It dawned on me at this point that I should have worn a ski mask, if such things even existed in southern Mexico. Some pantyhose would have also worked, or even a bandana tied around my face. There were a million things I could have used. It was such an incredibly stupid oversight. What else hadn't I thought of?

Too late now. Ten feet away, I stopped. Somehow the trio hadn't heard my footsteps, nor the deafening sounds of my own heartbeat.

"Hey…" I said, voice sounding different, like it wasn't my own.

They turned around and looked at me: random white dude, side of the road, middle of nowhere. A moment later they noticed the pistol in my hand. Hands went up without me having to ask.

"Go," I said, gesturing towards a narrow path leading into the woods. They didn't question this, just started walking, all three telling me how happy they'd be to hand over whatever I wanted—luggage, money, anything. No problem. And they'd forget all about this little incident once they got out of here. Water under the bridge. No cops, no embassy, no nothin'. They promised. No worries, man. All good.

I didn't respond to any of this, though part of me did wonder how much I'd be able to squeeze out of their families. A few grand? Twenty thousand? A hundred?

The plan was to march them into the woods and force them to confess to what they'd done—all while recording their confessions on my phone. Unfortunately, I hadn't thought about what I was going to say to elicit these confessions. Had all those episodes of *Law & Order* distorted my perception of how difficult this was going to be? (Suspects always confess on that show. *Always*.)

"Okay, stop here," I said, unsure what would come next.

They stopped.

"Turn around."

They did. The two sidekicks' faces were streaked with tears, but the ringleader looked pissed off more than anything.

"What are your names?"

Square Face went first: "Brody."

Of course his name was Brody. Travis and Chad were the other two. Straight out of central casting.

"You guys got anything you'd like to get off your chests?"

They looked at each other.

"Nothing?"

The runt of the bunch, Travis, spoke up. "What do you mean?"

"Some things you boys have gotten into these past few days. Anything come to mind?"

Their eyes darted to the ground, then over at each other.

"Come down to Mexico and do whatever you want, it don't matter. Anything goes, right?"

"I don't know what you're—" Brody started.

"Shut the fuck up." Whatever anxiety I'd been experiencing earlier had since transformed into anger. "How about we start with last night? What'd you get into after you ran into Javy at the bar?"

A look of recognition flashed across their faces: I was the guy from last night, their surf instructor's friend.

Brody took a step towards me. "Listen…"

I lifted the Colt .38 Super—brown handle, silver body, nine-round magazine plus one in the chamber—and pointed it at him. "Get down. On your knees, all of you."

The words were just coming out of my mouth at this point, though for a brief moment a thought did occur to me: *What the hell am I doing?*

All three, down on their knees. Chad and Travis put their hands on their heads for good measure, without me having to ask.

"You're going to tell me *exactly* what happened, okay?"

I slowly walked down the row, just a couple feet away from them. I held out the pistol, pointing it at each of their faces for a brief moment.

One.

Two.

Three.

I'd lost my fucking mind.

Tears were streaming down their faces now, even Brody's. Anything left in their bladders was released. What these guys didn't know was that I'd never shot anything in my life, and that I had no plans of starting tonight. Only reason I had the gun in the first place was because some slightly unhinged expats had convinced me years ago that I needed one "just in case." A couple hundred bucks later, I became an unregistered gun owner. (Even though the penalties for having an illegal firearm in Mexico were fucking *harsh*—much more severe than those in the United States.)

Phone in my pocket—battery 93% full, audio recorder on—the only thing I wanted from them was a confession. Would it be permissible in court?

Probably not, but it would at least get an investigation going, and maybe then they wouldn't be able to escape back up to the States so easily. It might have been a long shot, but it was better than letting them walk free.

"If you guys don't start talking," I said, shaking my head like the lunatic I was, "this isn't going to end well."

Chad wanted to talk. So did Travis. But even now, with a madman pointing a gun at their faces, they still looked to Brody for guidance. He'd somehow regained some of his inner fortitude after my little spiel. Maybe he'd seen through my bullshit tough guy routine? Up close to the guy, it was jarring to see how ugly he was, which was probably where he ran into problems with women. He was muscular, tan, and had a good head of hair—but all that shit only looked good from afar. His eyebrows were too thick, his eyes too close together. His nose: massive. His forehead: also massive.

"I'm going to ask again," I said, stopping in front of the caveman. "I already know about the girls. You know that in particular, motherfucker. But now you're going to tell me what happened last night."

"At the bar?" he asked.

"Don't play dumb."

"We didn't—"

"Brody," said one of the underlings, breaking rank. "Shut up."

I turned and faced him. "What happened?"

The kid was on the verge of a nervous breakdown.

"Travis, right?"

He managed a nod.

"Why don't you just tell me, my dude? And then we can all go our merry way…" I was talking like an idiot, like some bit character on a shitty police procedural (no TV shows come to mind).

"We were…" He stopped himself, eyes darting over towards Brody.

"Don't worry about him," I said. "Brody don't have a gun right now, does he?"

Fully in character now, I put the gun against Travis's throat. Either I was method acting or I'd *truly* lost my fucking mind.

"Last night— we didn't—"

Something flashed to my left.

Brody.

His arm came up and hit my hand, causing the pistol to move away from Travis's neck.

What it also did: caused my finger to spasm. To contract, to pull—to *something*.

The gun went off.

The bullet didn't go through the center of Travis's neck, but it did hit something else: his fucking *jugular*. He was covered in blood in an instant. So much blood. He fell backwards, clutching at his throat. Before I could react or think or do much of anything, Brody and Chad were up and running, away from the road, deeper into the woods.

It didn't occur to me to chase after them or yell at them to stop, and by the time it dawned on me that I could try to help Travis, it was already too late.

A minute later Mateo appeared next to me.

"*¿Qué pasó*?" he asked. Then he looked down. "*Dios mío...*"

He spun around, hands on his head. After muttering a quick prayer, he said, "Where are the other two?"

I gestured with the gun. "Somewhere…"

Mateo said a few more prayers while I just stood there, looking down at what I'd done. At the human being I'd just killed.

"What should we do?" he asked.

It took me a while to come up with an answer: "I have no idea."

FIVE

I woke up the next morning and enjoyed a few seconds of hopeful, ignorant bliss. It's that brief period immediately after opening your eyes, when you think all those images in your head are just leftover remnants of a bad dream. But you do eventually come around. Reality sets in. *No, no, these are real. These are memories.* I wasn't watching a bad movie play out in my head. I was just remembering yesterday, when I shot a person in the neck and watched as he bled out at my feet.

And the two other guys were still out there somewhere. There was a chance they'd traveled so deep into wilderness that no one would ever see them again (Starve to death? Bitten by a snake? Eaten by a puma?), but there was also a chance they'd stumbled across a road and made their way back to civilization. To a police station somewhere.

It was an accident. I didn't want to shoot *anything*, let alone a person. I should have taken out the magazine, emptied the chamber. It was idiotic that I hadn't. I'd never been a fan of guns—never wanted one—but then I let some delusional expats convince me that I was crazy *not* to have one, especially since I sometimes traveled alone along the coast, camping out beside my truck.

"What happens if you come across some *banditos*?" they'd ask, these overly fearful white Americans that—unfortunately—made up a sizable percentage of the expat community in southern Mexico.

"I don't know, I'll probably just—"

"You need a gun, Tony."

"I don't like guns."

"You need one."

"They make me uncomfortable."

A few weeks after this conversation, during one of my little surf safaris, I was heading out towards a right-hand point break when I came across a felled tree blocking the way (rarely traveled road, not much around). I knew right away. It took three guys just a couple of minutes to get everything they wanted from me: cash, phone, credit cards, drugs. The whole ordeal was surprisingly cordial. They didn't take my boards—too cumbersome to carry, most likely—and for some reason didn't take my truck either. They just disappeared back into the surrounding wilderness.

After that I turned around and headed to a different beach, to a place that wasn't so remote. I surfed at sunset, smoked a joint (they didn't find everything), and slept in the bed of my truck. After a quick session at dawn the next morning, I called my bank from a gas station and had some money wired to me. A few days later, after a couple of drunken conversations, I became the reluctant owner of a Colt .38 Super. My hope was that I'd never have to touch the thing, and up until yesterday, I hadn't.

No más.

☼

Awake, lying in bed, staring at the ceiling.

But also back in the woods, dead body at my feet. It wasn't until Mateo asked "What should we do?" that I was able to shake myself from the trance that had fallen over me. That I was able to think about what I'd done, and also what I hadn't.

What I *did* do: kill someone.

What I *did not* do: chase after the two guys—the two *witnesses*—that had run off into the woods. What I would have done once I caught up to them, I don't know. Shoot them? No way. Or: probably not. Or: who the fuck knows? Mateo and I did eventually start walking after them, but it only took a couple of minutes to realize that such efforts would be futile—they were younger, faster, and had a head start. They were long gone.

Back again at ground zero, it seemed like Travis's body had changed significantly in the five minutes we'd been gone, transforming from a human being I couldn't believe was dead to a corpse I couldn't believe had ever been alive. Mateo crouched down and inspected the ground around the body. I just stared at him for a while, wondering what the hell he was doing (*another* prayer?), until I remembered the pistol in my hand, and the bullet that had come out of it. It took some time, but he found the shell, and I found the casing.

"¿Vamos?"

"¿El cuerpo?" I asked. *"¿Qué hacemos?"*

In the brief conversation that ensued, we concluded that if we messed with the scene any further—with the body, in particular—we'd only end up leaving more evidence behind. We'd also get his blood all over us. For the time-being, we'd just leave it—we'd leave *him*. We'd come back later—or, maybe we'd come back later. We didn't know what the hell we were doing, to be honest, and there's a strong possibility we settled on this particular course of action (inaction?) due to one of the more basic human desires: to *not* have to deal with something.

We got back in the van and rode out to a small town located about halfway between Puerto

Escondido and Punta Cita. We drove around until we found an unsanctioned landfill, where we put the three backpacks into a rusted trash bin and added some cardboard and gasoline. Then we lit a match and watched the fire burn. We did that a few times.

Back in the van, Mateo flipped on the radio. Some old-school *música norteña* played, heavy on the accordion. I tried following along with the lyrics as a way to distract myself from what I'd just done, but this didn't work very well.

Mateo slowed to a stop about a half-mile outside of Punta Cita. No one was around: cars, people. "Maybe it's best if you don't get seen coming back with me."

My mind was so fixated on what just happened that I hadn't thought of this. Hadn't thought of anything really, other than Travis's dead body staring up at me.

"Tienes razón."

I got out and shut the door, then looked across at Mateo through the rolled-down window.

"Gracias," I said. It was all I could think to say.

"Estamos en esto juntos," he said. "And you should get rid of that gun. Wipe it down first."

Something else I'd somehow managed to forget: the gun tucked into my waistband. Ho hum, no big deal, just the fucking murder weapon. After he drove away, I looked around at my surroundings, trying to take in every last detail: curve of the road, potholes, trees that stood out. Once I thought I had a decent mental image of the place, I fought my way through thick brush until I was about a hundred feet away from the road. I looked around for a spot that would be easy to remember. This proved difficult—everything looked the same to me—but eventually I settled on a small clearing in front of an especially large tree.

I took the gun from my waistband and started wiping it down with my shirt. I wiped and wiped and wiped, then put it into a plastic bag I'd found alongside the road. I dug a hole beside the tree and dropped the bag inside. Then I filled the hole back in, patted down the dirt, and arranged three rocks on top of it, each about the size of my fist.

I stood up and looked down at my handiwork, pausing for a moment to contemplate: *What the hell am I doing?*

But I didn't have time to dwell on this question. I also didn't want to. I made my way back out to the road, where I looked around at my surroundings one last time before getting started on the mile-long trek back into town. When I glanced down and realized I was covered in dirt, I tried wiping myself off, but this only resulted in black streaks all over my body.

"For fuck's sake…"

If anyone saw me on the way back to my place, they'd have no choice but to ask what the hell I'd been doing. *Funny you ask…*

All I wanted to do was go home—without running into anyone—and take a shower. And then, of course, I'd smoke two-and-a-half joints and drink an entire bottle of tequila.

I'd just about made it—I was *almost* there—when I heard someone call out my name.

"Tony! Hey, man!"

Fuck me.

Fortunately, this voice had come from somewhere behind me. I could ignore it. I could just keep walking. Maybe they'd give up, and I could avoid this interaction.

"Tony! Hey!"

Again: *fuck me.*

I kept going. Faster now.

"Tony! Wait up!"

Jesus fucking Christ…

I stopped, closed my eyes, and told myself to relax. Didn't work.

I turned around to find Walt Hereford jogging towards me, a visual that actually did help me relax some. It was probably the first time in my life I'd ever been happy to see the idiot. Walt was a Canadian expat around my age who'd been in Punta Cita as long as I had—but the similarities ended there, thank god. He was a few inches shorter than me and had the build of someone who ate every single tortilla that came with his meals (in Mexico, this is problematic). He'd been living in Calgary until he attended a friend's February wedding in Cancún, which made him think that maybe he'd spent enough winters in Alberta. A few months after that he moved to Punta Cita and started a charter fishing company. Even though he wasn't that knowledgeable out on the water (he'd been an insurance agent in Calgary), his equipment was so much nicer than that of the local competitors, he got customers on that basis alone (first-timers only—he never got repeats).

"Dude, I just heard," he said, reaching out and putting his hand on my shoulder. "Fucking brutal, man."

"It is," I said. "Yeah."

"Any idea who did it?"

So people already knew: Javy's death was no accident. Punta Cita's a small town. Word travels fast.

"I don't," I said. "But hopefully the cops figure it out soon."

"Let me buy you a beer." He squeezed my shoulder. "Hell, however many you want. We're sharing Javy stories over at Barco, sort of like an Irish funeral."

El Barco Blanco was similar to La Hija's in that it was an open-air bar just off the beach, except Barco was on the opposite end of Calle Dorado, closer to the resorts. Its prices were higher, and so too was the percentage of its patrons classifiable as non-Hispanic white. (The English translation of the place: The White Boat.) The bar was the clichéd expat hangout in Punta Cita, which was precisely the reason I never went there.

"Thanks, man, but I'm just gonna head home. Not really feeling up for it."

"You sure?" The smell of booze on his breath was strong. This wasn't uncommon. In fact, it would have been weird if his breath didn't smell like a stale bottle of whiskey.

"I'm good. But thanks, man."

If anyone was going to see me in my current state, Walt was probably my best option. He was so drunk there was little chance he'd remember anything—

seeing me, talking to me, time of day, day of the week, his own goddamn name. He didn't even ask about the dirt all over my clothes.

I took a long shower when I got home. Afterwards, I put my clothes into a small chimenea out on my back patio. I lit that, then a joint. Tequila wasn't going down very well, so I settled for about a dozen beers instead. I sat out back, smoking and drinking in silence. Eventually I made my way to bed, which was where I woke up the next morning and experienced those few seconds of blissful, misguided hope.

Maybe it was just a bad dream…

It was not.

☼

I stumbled out of bed, put some clothes on, and made my way over to La Panadería de Arturo. The hangover was severe, and the smell of food only made things worse. I ordered a coffee and sat at a small table near the front, away from the kitchen. I stared out the window for a long time.

Why'd I come here?

Why'd I even get out of bed?

I finished the coffee and ordered another. I'd just sat back down at the table when I saw a pair of guys half-walking, half-jogging down Calle Dorado: dirty and haggard, eyes nearly bugging out of their heads. If I didn't know any better, I would have assumed they were just a couple of junkies (meth heads, most likely) in desperate need of a fix.

On my feet.

Out the door.

They were moving fast, so it didn't take long until they reached the police station. I stood there for a moment after they went inside, just staring at the station: dumbfounded, unbelieving.

A moment later I was hurrying back to my place. Even started into a little jog. I rushed into the kitchen, bent over at the sink, and splashed water on my face. Rubbed hands over a beard I didn't know I had.

I could book a flight—today—and fly into O'Hare. Easy. A couple of clicks, I'm there.

Or I could stick around and lie, say I'd never met Travis. Never seen him before.

I could even tell the truth—about how it was really *Brody's* fault, that it was *him* who had reached out and hit my hand and caused the gun to go off.

Maybe, also, I could just wait it out, see how things played out. This was my general approach to life: to *not* do anything until it became unavoidable. But given the circumstances here, I wasn't sure this was a great option. It might have worked in the past when it came to *not* having tough conversations in relationships and *not* quitting jobs I hated, but the current situation was different. I had *killed* somebody, and the two people who watched me do so were currently in the police station, presumably telling Gilberto all about it.

So: I needed to be proactive. I needed to do something.

But: *what?* I'd already gotten rid of the murder weapon (kind of), which was good, but maybe I should also get rid of something else? It's a dark place you go to, once you start thinking about how you might dispose of a human body. But... off I went.

Bury it deep in the woods somewhere? Take it out on a boat and tie a cinder block to its feet? I didn't have a boat, but I did have some matches and gasoline, and— *dear god what is wrong with me?* The place only gets darker once you start asking yourself the more detailed questions: Do human bones burn like wood? How much gasoline would I need? What kind of container? *Jesus Christ.* I couldn't do that. I couldn't *burn* a body.

But I could bury it. Yes. I could bury *him*.

Suddenly I felt this overwhelming urge to go back out to the body. It was like a countdown had started: I didn't know how much time was left, only that a clock was ticking. While part of me recognized how terrible of an idea it was to return to the scene of the crime—given that the two other bros were now back in town, it was probably the last thing I should have been considering—I was basically a runaway train at this point.

Out to my truck. Key. Ignition. Drive. Reason be damned.

I traveled slowly through town, smiling and waving at anyone who might get asked at a later date whether Tony Winslow seemed nervous or jumpy on this particular day. *Actually, he seemed way too happy. I mean, he's really not that pleasant of a dude when he's sober, and then all of a sudden—he's smiling, he's waving. So yeah, right away I knew something was up.*

I'd driven on plenty of bad roads since moving to Mexico, but never before had they seemed *this* bad. Every pothole was a personal affront, each one strategically located for the sole purpose of slowing me down. Twenty agonizing minutes later, I was there. No one was around: people, cars, nothing. I got out and ran into the woods, carrying three things with me: a trash bag, latex gloves, and a shovel. Nothing suspicious at all. Not sketchy. Totally normal. As I made my way along the narrow path, I pictured the guys from the day before, marching in front of me, kneeling down, crying, begging, pissing their pants.

And the shot. The accident. Yes, god damn it—the *accident!* This was an important word. I didn't fire the gun again when Square Face and Chad ran off, deeper into the woods. Didn't even think to do so, and this was both a good and bad thing. The good: killing one person was better than killing three people. The bad: having two eyewitnesses was worse than having zero eyewitnesses.

Once I made it out to the clearing—the scene of the *accident*—I noticed something strange: the body wasn't there. There was dirt and mud, bushes and trees. But no body. Nothing was red, either. There was no blood-soaked soil, no impressions left in the dirt. It almost seemed too natural, like someone had gone to great lengths to make it look like nothing had happened here.

I spun around, looking left, right, everywhere. The pulse in my head was deafening. Each heartbeat felt like a tremor.

Maybe it really had been a dream? Is that what happened? Maybe the joint I smoked the day before had been laced with PCP? The drug *was* pretty popular in the neighboring town of Pucerías, so this wasn't an entirely implausible scenario (even though I'd been buying from the same guy for years and rolled the joint myself). I looked around some more, then sat down on a rock. A few seconds later it dawned on me: I was in the wrong spot.

I jumped up and ran back out to my truck, driving north, away from town. Whatever shocks remained on my red 2009 Ford Ranger ceased to exist after I hit a hundred potholes over the next five minutes.

I pulled over: *this* was the spot. I raced into the woods until I came to a clearing.

Nothing.

I repeated this process a third time, then a fourth, until eventually I resigned myself to one of two possibilities: I'd either forgotten where the accident had taken place or someone had beaten me to the spot. Brody and Chad retracing their steps? Had they led cops out to the body?

At this point I started wondering how much of a learning curve there would be for Mexican prison slang. Or would I get extradited back to the United States? (Not many *Law & Order* episodes had an international slant, so I was lost here.)

Standing on the side of the road beside my truck, I contemplated driving north, to one of the many small towns nestled in the mountains. I'd lay low, hide out for a little while. A few weeks, a few years. However long was needed. Or I could drive to the airport and book that flight to Chicago, go hike the Pacific Crest Trail or some shit.

But neither option felt right—what I was basing this on, I don't know—so I drove south, back towards Punta Cita. Back at my place, my first two orders of business were packing a bowl and then finding my lighter. Right before I was about to get to work, I stopped and looked around. Something seemed off. I started walking around, slowly.

Bedroom: clothes all over the floor, bed unmade.

Bathroom: dirty but not filthy.

Kitchen: lots of dishes, little food.

In other words: everything was normal. The most likely explanation for the weird vibes was that I'd simply lost my mind. I grabbed a bottle of tequila from the freezer and poured myself a double. I then grabbed my bong and went out on the back patio, where it smelled, oddly, like cigarette smoke. Save for a brief phase in high school during which I thought smoking menthols might help me get laid (it did not), I'd never been a smoker (this was one of the few good decisions I'd made in my life).

"Tony, *¿qué pasa?*" said Gilberto, as if nothing at all was strange about him being on my patio. He was smoking a cigarette and sitting in one of the two plastic chairs I had out back. *How did he get inside? And how the hell had he managed to squeeze himself into that chair?*

"It was unlocked," he said, answering the first of the two without me having to ask.

Maybe here's when I should have acted like some indignant tough guy. *What right do you have to be in my house!* At least then it wouldn't have seemed like I was almost expecting him to be there.

But I didn't say anything. Not a word. I just stood there, double of tequila in one hand, bong in the other.

"I think we need to talk," he said.

I took a seat in the other plastic hair. I set my bong on the ground and drank down the tequila, wishing afterwards that I'd given myself a healthier pour.

SIX

Gilberto had this way of saying things without actually saying them. It's a necessary skill for a dirty cop: being able to get a point across without being explicit, so if some Internal Affairs investigator ever listened in on one of his conversations, there wouldn't be anything that jumped out as inappropriate or suspicious. Thanks to this innate ability of his—and also his position of relative power—Gilberto did pretty well for himself. Big house, nice car.

But they could always be bigger, nicer.

Truth is, the unofficial bribery system in Mexico isn't too different than the legal system in the United States: the more money you have, the better off you'll be. More money up in the States means you can afford bail, competent lawyers, and charges conveniently getting dropped. Things are just a bit more direct in Mexico: you pay the people investigating, and if that doesn't work, you pay a prosecutor, or a judge, or everyone on the goddamn jury.

For a brief moment he and I just sat there on the patio, listening to the faint sounds of waves breaking in the distance. The negotiations were underway—he'd started the process by coming to my house, and now it was my move. The main issue for me was that I didn't know what Brody and Chad had already told him, though I could safely assume it involved a flat tire, a roadside bandito, and a dead travel companion.

What'd the bandito look like?

Mid-40's, white guy. Black hair and beard, little gray in both.

Hold on. A white *guy? You sure?*

Yeah, he accused us of killing Javy, the surf instructor.

So he spoke English?

Yeah.

How good?

Like a native.

Like an American?

I think he was *American.*

And he just came out of the woods?

Yeah.

It's just— I've never in my— a gringo bandito?

If this had been the basic gist of their conversation (and what else could it have been?), Gilberto probably knew right away the identity of this gringo bandito. And while there was little doubt the two bros could have picked me out of a lineup, they didn't know my name, where I lived, or anything about me. This gap in their knowledge was my saving grace. It was also where Gilberto had identified a money-making opportunity.

But one person the bros *could* identify: Mateo. I hadn't even considered what the two guys showing up meant for him, though it didn't take me long to reach a conclusion here: he was fucked. He'd picked them up, driven them around in circles, and then let some random dude march them off into the woods at gunpoint—and then he never mentioned a word about it to his boss, police, anyone. How had we forgotten to come up with such an essential part of his cover story? What else had we forgotten? What else hadn't we considered?

Demoralizing as this realization was, I'd have to worry about Mateo later. Right now I had to focus on my own survival. I had to make sure the next several minutes of conversation didn't involve me confessing, signing over the deed to my house, or transferring the entirety of my savings account over to Gilberto.

"You know," he said, finally breaking the silence, since I seemed incapable of doing so. "This is going to get a lot of attention."

"What do you mean?"

He laughed. "A tourist from the States disappears..."

Disappears?

"...his friend and his brother claim he was killed, but not by a Mexican..."

They claim *he was killed. So they don't have a body?*

"...or some narco. Nope. Guess who they say killed him?"

"Who?"

The grin on his face was beyond arrogant at this point. "They say it was some middle-aged white guy."

"Is that right?"

"Not what you'd expect, right?"

I shrugged. "Probably not, no."

"People from Mexico City will fly in to work on this. They'll want it closed fast. You can get away with lots of things, but once you start scaring off tourists..." He took one last drag on his cigarette, then tossed the butt into my chimenea. "So if you're involved in this somehow, Tony, I can assure you that you're better off dealing with me than someone from Mexico City. *¿Me entiendes?*"

"What do you mean?" I asked, more committed to playing dumb than I'd realized. "I don't know what you're implying here—"

He laughed. "I get it. You're not ready. *Está bien.* But don't wait until it's too late."

Then began the arduous process of him getting up from the white plastic chair. (Plastic may very well be destroying the planet, but god damn if it isn't a miracle material.)

"You know where to find me," he said, once he'd finally made it to his feet. Then he walked inside, out through the front door.

I stayed where I was, mind a jumbled mess. Getting out of Mexico seemed like a good idea, but wouldn't running be the most guilty-looking thing I could do? Wouldn't that be the equivalent of admitting that I was guilty of *something?* Which, of course, I was. And what about extradition? How the hell did all that work?

But running away wasn't an option for Mateo, a man who didn't think twice when I asked him if he could do me a "little favor." I couldn't just leave him on his own to deal with this. But what could I do to help him? I didn't know, but just bailing on the guy—someone with a wife and *six* kids—just didn't seem right.

It felt like my head was about to explode, which actually wouldn't have been the worst of things. I walked inside, swallowed some more tequila. Then I grabbed a beer and walked back outside, where I kicked the chair I'd been sitting in.

"Fuck!" I screamed, before pacing back and forth for a while.

Eventually I sat down in the other plastic chair, where right away I finished off the job I could only assume Gilberto had started: the back legs snapped underneath me. I fell backwards, head smacking against the cement patio. It was a pretty solid jolt but not enough for me to lose consciousness. Shame. I didn't have the wherewithal to protect my head during the fall, but I did manage to keep my beer upright.

Since I was already down on the ground, I just laid there for a while, staring up at the sky. I drank the beer while contemplating never again getting up. Maybe I could just lay there and drink beer until the end of time? But how could I drink any more without first getting up to go grab some more? This was a problem of mine, not seeing the glaring holes in my stupid fucking plans.

☼

Ten minutes later I was on my feet, inside. I took a piss (the main reason for getting up) then grabbed some deli meat from the fridge (turkey, I think; unexpired, I think), which I doused with mustard and shoved into my mouth. I swallowed before I could taste anything. After that, I set off towards Vicente's. I figured I'd check in with him, see if he'd heard anything. Even though he rarely left his outpost, he always seemed to be the first to know about anything happening in town.

I nearly shit myself when the bar came into sight, and it wasn't because of the mystery deli meat I'd just eaten (maybe it wasn't turkey; maybe, also, it had expired). Mateo was there. Just sitting at the bar, drinking a beer. *How has he not been arrested?* It dawned on me a moment later that just because I hadn't thought up a good cover story didn't mean he hadn't.

I sat down next to him. *"Mateo, hombre, ¿cómo estás?"*

"Todo bien, todo bien."

Vicente slid over a Pacífico.

"Did you talk to Gilberto?" I asked, after Vicente had walked towards the other end of the bar.

"Sí, más temprano."

"What'd you say?"

"That I got a flat, and next thing I know, some guy comes out and marches the passengers off into the woods. Then I heard a shot and drove away."

It wasn't a terrible story, I had to admit. But there were some holes.

"Why didn't you call the cops?"

"No service."

"Why didn't you say anything when you got back?"

"He threatened me before running off into the woods. Said he'd kill my family."

"Jesus…"

"Todo bien, hombre."

"But what about their luggage?"

"I didn't shut the door before driving away, so it must've fallen out somewhere along the way."

I took a long pull from the Pacífico, feeling dizzy all of a sudden. Was I drunk? Stoned? Concussed from my fall? Or was it simply excitement that I was feeling? Were we—both of us, me *and* Mateo—in the clear here? Sure, some bribes would still be necessary, but that was just part of doing business.

"All good at the resort?"

"*Pues,* no, I got fired."

"What?" Had I misheard him? Was I missing something? "You just said everything was good."

"It is."

I looked at him for a long moment. "But… you lost your job."

"There are other ones."

"How could they fire you if the police cleared you?"

He laughed. "Worried about their TripAdvisor reviews, I guess."

"Seriously?"

"It's not like there's a union over there. They do what they want." He shrugged, drank his beer. "Again: there are other jobs."

He was right, but no other job in Punta Cita would be nearly as comfortable as shuttle bus driver for La Vista del Mar. Sitting down for four to eight hours each day was as close to Mateo's dream job as he was ever going to get—and that was before we even considered the beers he was able to sneak in throughout the day.

"I'll be fine," he said. "*No te preocupes.*"

"Jesus, man. If there's anything I can do, just… god damn it. I'm sorry I dragged you into this, I shouldn't have—"

"Don't apologize," he said, gesturing at Vicente to bring us two more beers. "He deserved what came to him. My only regret is that we let the other two get away."

The look in his eyes made one thing clear: he wasn't some fake tough guy, talking out of his ass here. He was serious.

"Have you been back out to the spot?" I asked, once Vicente was out of earshot again, even though the old guy had sponges for ears and had probably heard every word we'd said so far.

"*Claro que no*," said Mateo, and then he looked over at me like I was an idiot. "Have *you*?"

"Kind of."

"What the hell, Tony?"

"I know, it was stupid. But I'm not sure I was even at the right place."

"What do you mean?"

"I couldn't find it."

"The spot? Or the body?"

"Both, or— well, I'm not sure…" I described where I'd gone. Road, landmarks, everything. He said that sounded about right, but he couldn't be sure.

"I don't know how I missed it."

"Probably for the best."

Over the course of a few more beers, I told Mateo I'd help him out with whatever he needed—finding a job, paying bills, anything. He kept telling me not to worry, *todo bien, no te preocupes*. His attitude didn't make any sense to me, but I didn't feel like arguing with him. I put some pesos on the bar and started back towards my place. I'd just about made it home when Walt Hereford came rushing up to me.

"Tony!" he called out, and these two syllables were all I needed to know that he was sloshed. "What the fuck's going on around here?"

I didn't stop walking as Walt ran through the new gossip: two American tourists were claiming their brother/friend was shot and killed by some white guy. But—*but!*—the police couldn't find the body.

"There's no body?"

"No body."

"Are you sure?"

"That's what I heard. But I'm wondering if maybe it's the same guy who killed Javy."

"I don't know—"

He grabbed my arm, jumped in front of me. His eyes were the size of grapefruits. "Has to be, right?"

"Maybe," I said. "But what's the connection?"

"Murders on back-to-back days. Tony, man," he said, shaking his head, "there's no way they're *not* related."

"I guess..." I moved to walk past him, but he took a step, blocking my way.

"Let me buy you a beer. You look like shit."

"It's been a rough few days."

"Come on, first couple of rounds are on me."

"Not tonight."

"And you know I always got some candy."

"I'm good."

Even if circumstances had been different, no amount of free booze and cocaine would have made hanging out with Walt Hereford worth the annoyance.

"Hope you feel better, man," he said, squeezing my arm before stumbling his way back to, most likely, Barco Blanco. Walt was fucked up more often than not, but over the past few days he seemed to have taken his debauchery to a whole new level. Not that I had much room to talk. Or: any room to talk.

☼

"Did you do it?"

Kerstin. Arms crossed, standing by my front gate. I really needed to stop staring down at the ground as I walked.

"Hey," I said, after too long of a pause. "Do what?"

"Did you?"

"Did I what?"

"Don't play dumb."

"Kerstin..." I said, reaching for her hand. "I don't—what are you talking about?"

She pulled her arm back. "Do *not* touch me. I can't believe… I can't…" She put a hand to her face. Chin starting to wobble, tears welling in her eyes. "Do *not…*"

"Listen…" I said, though I had no clue what to say after this. "It's…"

She looked at me, waiting for me to say the words she knew to be true. She'd heard the gossip. She'd connected the dots. It was pretty simple, really.

But I couldn't do it. I couldn't tell her.

"It wasn't me," I said. "I swear."

She stared at me for a long moment, then walked away.

SEVEN

A few days passed. The weather was perfect, the way it always is in Oaxaca (during the dry season, at least), which can be fairly annoying when you're not in a good mood yourself. Sometimes you just need a few clouds. I spent the majority of these days pacing around my house: eating canned goods, drinking beer, smoking pot. I tried distracting myself (books, TV, music), but mostly I remained stuck in an endless loop of regret and self-loathing. I thought a lot about how I should have settled down years ago, in some suburb outside of Chicago: Green Oaks, Lincolnshire, wherever. But I could never bring myself to pull the trigger on that kind of lifestyle, in part because I was fearful I'd pull the non-metaphorical kind shortly thereafter.

However, if I *had* given it a go, instead of eating expired deli meat, navy beans, and stale tortillas on a regular basis (and boozing so much that dialysis will be needed at some point), I could have been living in a four-bed, two-and-a-half-bath house in the Midwest. I could have worn a suit Monday through Thursday then dressed down on Fridays, casual but not too casual. Also on Fridays: pizza nights. I'd pick up a few overpriced pies on the way home, from the kind of place that doesn't shut the fuck up about being farm-to-table adjacent. After eating with the kids (and a few of their friends?), my wife and I would share a moderately priced bottle of wine, then fall asleep on the couch as we watched some terrible show on Netflix. She'd wake up around midnight and nudge me to come up to bed with her, but I'd feign some deep, otherworldly exhaustion and stay down on the couch. I'd always preferred sleeping by myself. Falling asleep alone, waking up alone—there's something nice about that, something natural.

So, it's probably a good thing, me ending up alone in a little casita in Oaxaca, though it wasn't like there weren't small houses up in the U.S., cheap acres to be had somewhere out in Arizona, Idaho, Montana, places where I wouldn't have had to try for some fucked-up version of vigilante justice.

The thing that eventually forced me to leave my house was the paddle-out for Javy, which is basically surfing's version of a memorial service. Though I'd been expecting a large crowd, the actual turnout far exceeded my expectations. It seemed like every surfer in southern Mexico had shown up. There was also a large crowd on the beach, including quite a few women with tears streaming down their faces. I didn't doubt the genuineness of these emotions, but I did suspect that there might have been some sort of unspoken competition taking place: who was the *most* upset? (Even after his death, the bastard had women fighting over him.)

"Look at this crowd," said Walt, walking beside me as we both carried boards out to the water. He didn't surf, but like many others, he'd either borrowed or rented a board in order to take part in the ceremony. "I hope they catch whoever—"

"Me too," I said, hopping onto my longboard and immediately paddling away from him.

☼

Carlita held the after-party at La Hija's. Everyone knew the story at this point: Javy had confronted a few guys the night he died, accusing them of having sexually assaulted two local women. Everyone had their own theories regarding the identities of these women. All were incorrect.

Marysol, Paloma, and Luisa weren't at the paddle-out (I didn't see them, anyway), but they did make it to La Hija's. They sat over in a corner, sipping waters and keeping mostly to themselves. After a few beers at the bar, I decided to walk over and sit down beside Marysol. Though she hadn't been assaulted, she wore the pain of the experience more visibly than the other two. We talked about the paddle-out, how nice it was to see a big crowd like this. Paloma and Luisa never engaged, eyes darting around at the crowd or down at the table, barely a word spoken between them. I asked how the fruit stand was doing. *Bien,* she said. Conversation wasn't coming easily (what did I expect?), and after a while the four of us just kind of sat there, staring off into the crowd. People were laughing and telling stories, about Javy doing this and that. A few of the more committed women continued with the tears, the winner of the competition yet to be determined.

"*¿Esto no es tu culpa, me entiendes*?" I said, finally getting the words out that I'd walked over here to say. I thought they needed to hear this, that Javy's death wasn't their fault.

Marysol looked away, into the crowd.

"*Mírame. Por favor.*"

It took some more pleading, but she did eventually look at me.

"*Por favor, mírame,*" I said. "*Paloma y Luisa, por favor.*"

They eventually did too, at which point I started off into my best impression of Robin Williams in *Good Will Hunting.*

"It's not your fault... *No es tu culpa... No es tu culpa...*"

They eventually humored me with some nods, but whether they believed me or not, I couldn't tell. Most likely they just wanted me to shut the hell up. I figured if I tried pushing any further, it would've been too aggressive (if it wasn't already), because not only am I *not* a trained therapist, but I'm also generally an idiot when it comes to interpersonal communication. After my impromptu, mostly plagiarized spiel, the four of us went back to just sitting in silence together. Didn't take long until I felt like a complete buffoon for having even attempted the pseudo therapy session. Before I could delve any further into this favorite rabbit hole of mine—*Reasons Why Tony Winslow is a Worthless Shitbag*—Marysol leaned over and said, "No one knows it was Paloma and Luisa that were..."

"I've never used your names," I said, which was mostly true. I'd only told Javy.

"*Bien, bien,*" she said. "It's just that we can't..."

Even with murder now added to the guys' rap sheets, she was still worried about coming forward, only to get sent back to Guatemala City, a place they'd fled because a gang member had developed a "romantic interest" in Paloma. Unless you're under the protection of another gang, it can be awfully dangerous to say no to these kinds of overtures. Some might even consider it suicidal. For many, then, the only option is to try to escape and build a life elsewhere. That's exactly what these women had done. And up until a week ago, things had been going pretty well.

"Entiendo," I said, standing up. *"Está bien."*

"And Tony," said Marysol. "What happened to the one guy? The one they say was shot."

I felt Paloma and Luisa's eyes on me. I looked at Marysol for a brief moment before saying, "I don't know anything about that."

She nodded. "I didn't think you would."

I fought my way through the crowd, put my empty can on the bar, and walked home. I tried making a few calls but no one answered. After the third failed attempt, I went out to my shed, pulled out my entire quiver, and then, one at a time, removed all of the old wax and put a new coat on each board. The whole process took a few hours, and though the un-waxing and re-waxing weren't necessary, it kept me occupied.

Later that night I laid in bed, listening to the waves in the distance, wondering what might have happened to the body of Travis McBride. Also on my mind: *Why the fuck isn't Gilberto answering my calls?*

☼

I paddled out the following morning, my first session in over a week. Sparse lineup, decent waves. After a couple of hours in the water, I was feeling pretty good. Great, even.

But then I wasn't, because on the three-minute walk back to my place I spotted Gilberto standing along Calle Dorado, chatting with Brody, Chad, and a white guy around my age. Fortunately—as in *thank fucking god*—they weren't looking in my direction. When Gilberto took a slight step to his right, a fifth member of the group became visible: some serious-looking dude with the Policía Federal Ministerial, Mexico's version of the FBI. He looked like the kind of guy who ate egg white omelets and ran half-marathons while on vacation.

I lowered my head and rushed home, trying to remain hidden behind my longboard. A quick Google search gave me all I needed: the white guy, Kevin McBride, was the father of Chad and Travis. The two "survivors" had traveled home during my weeklong hibernation, but now they were back, and they'd brought reinforcements. Not only was daddy now involved, but some members of the press had also made the trip down.

How I'd managed *not* to see this coming is a question with just one answer: I'm a fucking idiot. But now that the nightmare scenario was playing out, I really had no other options: I had to get out of town, at least for a little while.

I loaded my longboard into the bed of my truck then grabbed two other boards from the shed: a fish with some volume and a shortboard designed for a far better surfer than me. My plan was pretty straightforward: I'd make it look like I was going on a little surf trip. That was it. Simple. After strapping in my boards, I went inside and packed up the essentials: zinc oxide, a towel, my toothbrush, a bottle of tequila, rolling papers, filters, and every bit of pot I could find. Then, from the safe underneath my bed came the most important item: money. I put some American currency into my wallet and a much heftier sum into a blank envelope, one I found tucked away between *Desert Solitaire* and *Cosmic Banditos,* two books I also decided to pack along for the trip.

I locked the front door, shut the outer gate. Given recent history I fully expected Kerstin or Gilberto to be waiting out by my truck, ready to drop some bomb on me.

Tony, you're going to be a father.

Tony, you're under arrest for first-degree murder.

But neither showed up. No life sentence, at least not yet. I took a circuitous route around town, going nowhere near Calle Dorado, then circled back until I was about a mile outside the other side of Punta Cita. Gilberto had a house far too big for a humble public servant, so it wasn't hard to pick out. I put my truck in park and walked to the front gate. Before I could knock, a short, round woman opened the door a few inches, just enough so that I could see her face. Based on everything I'd heard about her, she was some combination of maid, concubine, and wife.

"Aqui tiene," I said, handing over the envelope. I could tell right away that she was used to this kind of thing—receiving envelopes full of cash—though maybe not something quite this thick. Given the presence of the PMF and all the media attention the case had received (which I'd been ignoring up to this point), I figured a hefty sum was my only hope of

staying out of the investigators' crosshairs. God knows I should've delivered the money earlier, but Gilberto hadn't been answering my calls, and I wasn't too comfortable with the idea of leaving a message. *Hey dude, about that bribe we talked about, how much you thinking?* Even now as I was handing over the money, I wasn't sure how long he'd be able to drag his feet on an investigation that would eventually point to me.

"From Tony Winslow," I said. "And it also covers Mateo Sandoval. *¿Está bien*?"

She nodded once before shutting the door in my face.

☼

I headed south on Carretera 200, sights set on Puerto Escondido. Windows down, Pacific Ocean to my right, I messed around with the radio until I found a station playing some old norteño music. I was tempted to stop at a roadside bar for a quick beer or two, but I figured the sooner I got out of the area, the better. The plan was to drive all the way through Mexico, and then Guatemala, El Salvador, Honduras. Final destination: Nicaragua. Not exactly the easiest road trip, but I knew quite a few people who'd made the journey without too many problems. (The piece of advice offered most frequently: *Don't drive at night. Like, ever.*) Once I got to Nica, I'd find a little place along the coast, somewhere that accepted cash and didn't require ID. I'd spend my days surfing and trying not to think too much about Travis McBride. I'd reread *East of Eden* and highlight my favorite passages in *Desert Solitaire*. I'd drink tequila and finish off the last of my bud, then ask a bartender where I could get some more, wholesale. I'd always heard that Nicaraguans were a friendly people, though I'd heard the same thing about the residents of every Central American country. Based on my experiences in the region, these were all true statements. Even though the country was currently going through what some might consider a bit of a political crisis, I figured I'd be all right. How bad could it be in some remote beach town? And as Vicente had told me years ago, "Every country in Latin America is either entering into or going through a crisis. There is no third option."

I was four hours past Puerto Escondido when I decided to stop for the night in Salina Cruz. I paid in cash at the Seaway Breeze and signed my name as Charlie Wilbury. I carried a few things into my room then walked to a roadside restaurant a block away, where I ate four fish tacos and drank three beers. Back in my room I turned on the TV and flipped through channels for a while, eventually settling on some old telenovela. I rolled a joint and smoked it down to the filter. I fell asleep shortly thereafter.

☼

The first thing I noticed when I woke up: unnaturally white teeth.

Some morning show on TV. Full heads of hair. Cleavage. Blinding smiles.

Second thing I noticed: the vibrating cell phone on the nightstand beside me. I picked up without looking.

"Hello?"

"Tony," said a female voice. "Where are you?"

"Kerstin?"

"Where are you? Are you okay?"

"I'm fine. What's up?"

"They arrested Mateo."

I jolted upright, blood rushing to my head, room going blurry. "For what?"

"His story didn't check out."

Heart sinking. Stomach sinking. Everything: *sinking*. "What do you mean?"

"There was no flat tire. The spare was still in the back of the van."

"Jesus Christ..." How *impossibly* stupid could we have been? All we had to do was take a knife to a tire and put the spare on—boom, there was our cover story. "Is he in jail?"

"Since last night. Yolanda came over to my place this morning, after she saw you weren't home. She was hoping you might have an idea about what to do."

"Fuck..." Six kids at home, her husband now in jail. How many lives had I ruined over these past few days? Had I set some sort of record?

"Why would she come looking for you?" asked Kerstin, after a moment.

The answer here was fairly obvious: Mateo had told his wife what happened.

"I'm not…" I stood up, started pacing. "I don't know why she'd… yeah, I don't know."

"There's only one reason, Tony…"

"Listen—"

"…and that's because you're involved."

"Kerstin, that's— it's not—"

"Did you kill that kid?"

"No," I said, emphatically. It was a weird sensation, being genuinely offended by an accurate accusation. "I didn't kill anybody."

"Then what happened?"

"I don't know, I don't— I just think we need to focus on how we can help Mateo right now."

The problem here—or, one of the many problems here—was that I had no idea how to do so. I also didn't know what he'd told police, and what that would mean for me if I went back to Punta Cita. Would I get brought in for questioning? Arrested? Thrown in jail?

"Where are you right now?"

"I gotta run," I said, hanging up before she could ask a follow-up.

I packed up my few things—boards, lighter, toothbrush, toothpaste—and walked out to my truck. I started the engine but didn't go anywhere for a while. I just sat there in the parking lot, staring at my dashboard. I could stick to the original plan and make my way to Nicaragua. Find a little town and hit the reset button. Start over. Again. Down south, just a little further down this time. Change my name to Charlie Wilbury and pay cash wherever I went. *Time to move on, time to get going, what lies ahead…*

I put the truck in reverse, started to back out.

A second later I was back in park. "God damn it…"

I wasn't "moving on." I was running away and leaving Mateo to sit in jail and cover for me. (I had a strong hunch that he'd mentioned my name to his wife, but not to the cops.) Plus, there was all the rest of Punta Cita I'd be leaving behind, a town where, in spite of myself, I'd managed to develop meaningful friendships with some kind, wonderful people. Not but a minute ago I was ready to flee—ready to disappear forever—yet now here I was, ashamed with myself for having even considered the option. Before my mind could wander back into a tangled mess of conflicting thoughts, I backed up and headed west, back towards Punta Cita. I drove with the windows down and radio up. Norteño music played. Bass, accordion, and love gone wrong.

EIGHT

It was late afternoon by the time I got back to Punta Cita. I'm not sure what I expected when I walked into the police station, but it certainly didn't involve Brody, Chad, and Kevin all sitting right there in the fucking lobby. Brody and Chad jumped up from their chairs as soon as they saw me, with the latter backing away and shrieking, "That's him! It's *him*!"

Brody, meanwhile, came towards me, and it didn't look like he wanted to shake hands. I'd never been much of a fighter, but anyone with eyes and a pulse could have seen that he was gearing up for a straight right. I ducked underneath the punch and came up with a right uppercut of my own, which found him square in his stomach. He bent over, gasping for air.

I should have left it at that.

I did not.

I put my hands on the back of his head and lifted my knee up to meet his face, which hurt my knee a lot more than I'd imagined. He crumpled to the floor, motionless.

Chad had positioned himself entirely behind his father by this point. He'd continued shrieking, though his outbursts were now largely unintelligible. The only other person in the room, a young woman who'd been sitting quietly behind a small desk, seemed amused more than anything. A few seconds later, Gilberto emerged from his office with orange crumbs all over his face (and also shirt). Cheetos? Doritos? I couldn't be sure.

"It's him!" screamed Chad, arm straight and stiff, finger pointed directly over at me. "He killed Travis!"

"Arrest him!" shouted Kevin McBride, finally finding his voice. "What the hell are you waiting for?"

Gilberto's English wasn't great, but I assumed he could understand the gist of the McBrides' outburst. As I stood over an unconscious Square Face, my thoughts danced back to the motel in Salina Cruz. I should have just kept driving, east and then south, all the way to Nica. How stupid was I? Not only to come back, but then to just *walk into the police station*. The fuck? And it wasn't like I'd returned because of honor or pride, or some other bullshit ideal. Hell no. It was just miscalculated self-interest. I didn't want to feel guilty for the rest of my life because I'd abandoned a good friend. I didn't want to carry that around with me. Now all that was left for me to do: spend the rest of my life in a jail cell, thinking about how nice it was to be guilt-free.

Gilberto just stood there staring at me for a brief moment. He seemed dumbfounded. Understandably.

"I don't know what they're talking about," I said to Gilberto, casually as I could manage while also being loud enough to cut through the chants of *Arrest him!*

"*¿Qué haces acá?*" he asked, eyes nearly bugging out of his head.

"Just wanted to see if there were any updates in the investigation into Javy Martinez's death."

Chad glanced away when I looked over at him, though he probably would have done so no matter what I'd said. *Merry Christmas. Happy Birthday. Peace be with you.* In his eyes, I was a murderous madman, and the scary truth was that he wasn't wrong.

Gilberto gestured for me to follow him back to his office. He also ordered a young cop to attend to Square Face, who was just now starting to come to. Though the temptation was there, I didn't kick him before turning around and following Gilberto. I considered this to be a good sign: my impulse control was improving.

☼

"*¿Qué carajos estás haciendo?*" said Gilberto, collapsing into the chair behind his desk.

"I'm not sure what they told you, but—"

"Shut the fucking door."

"Listen," I said, after following orders. "I don't know what they're—"

"Not only do you come *back* into town," he said, not the least bit interested in what I had to say. "But then you assault somebody *inside* a police station, a person who's accusing you of murder. Mind you, this person had no *fucking* idea what your name was or where you were until you just walked in here." He put a finger underneath the collar of his shirt (XXXL?) and pulled it away from his neck. His face was covered with sweat, much more than just its usual glisten. "Did I miss anything?"

After a moment: "So maybe this wasn't the best approach."

"You think?"

"What's the deal with Mateo?" I asked, trying to steer the conversation away from my own idiocy. "Is he in jail?"

"A story that revolves around a flat tire, except—get this—*there's no flat tire!* What the fuck am I supposed to do with that?"

"That's why I stopped by your house yesterday."

"You did no such thing," he said, eyes going wide.

"Maybe if you would've called me back, we could've talked about it."

"That's exactly why I *didn't* call you back. And that's also exactly why you're going to shut the fuck up right now. *Entendido*?"

I leaned back against the cement wall and closed my eyes. Somehow I fought off the urge to just start banging my head against the thing. "So where do we stand?"

"*We*?"

"Me and Mateo. What's the deal?"

"Mateo? He's fucked, and now you are too. That's the deal. All we had before you walked in here a few minutes ago was basically 'a gringo friend of Javy's.' That was fucking *it*. And everyone's friends with Javy! Now we have a face and a name, because for some reason you thought it'd be a good idea to come back into town, show up at the police station, and get into a fight."

In hindsight, the smart approach would have been to hang out in Nicaragua until all this blew over, or at least until the two witnesses who could identify me had left town. It was pretty straightforward, yet I'd somehow convinced myself that the only honorable thing to do was to return to Punta Cita right away (even though this was, again, just some miscalculated self-interest). Maybe I should have also considered this: I wouldn't be much help to Mateo if I was sharing a jail cell with him.

There was no way around it: I fucked up.

"What do you think I should do?"

"Do you have a time machine?" he said, looking at me like he actually wanted an answer to this. I stared down at my feet as he continued in a lower voice, "Some people from Mexico City have already come down. If you run now, you look guilty. Not saying you shouldn't, but that's sure as hell what it'll look like. And if you stay, you're going to have to do a lot of explaining."

"What about…" I started, before realizing I didn't have anything to offer. Thoughts, ideas, strategies. I had nothing.

"I could arrest you right now, Tony. I *should* arrest you right now. For the assault you just committed, and then I could hold you for questioning about the disappearance of Travis McBride."

"The assault was self-defense."

"What about Travis?"

I shrugged. "I don't know anything about that."

"If you stick around, I'm going to have to pull you in at some point. You know that, right?"

I nodded.

He let out a long breath. It was Doritos he'd been eating. Cool Ranch. "But I'm a man of my word, so I'll let you walk out of here. Once that happens, once you leave, we're even, *¿me entiendes?* It's not my fault you walked right the fuck back into this. But this will at least give you some time to talk to people: your lawyer, some diplomat, whoever."

Gilberto: a man of his word. I was tempted to laugh in his face and tell him to go fuck himself, except I knew I wasn't any better myself. Hell, I was worse. I lied every time I opened my mouth, and here I was using my gringo privilege to buy my way out of trouble. All because I'd been born to middle-class parents in a rich country. What a guy I was.

After exiting through the back, I put my head down and hurried back to my place, where I cracked open a Pacífico and rolled a joint. A few minutes later there was a knock at my door. After contemplating several options—escaping out the back; grabbing a knife and then opening the door; sitting still and pretending I wasn't home—I took a quick toke (also my first), stubbed out the joint, and peeked out the front window: Kerstin, standing out by my front gate. I wasn't sure what it was that I felt in this moment: happiness, relief, nervousness? Some combination? I walked outside and opened the gate.

She held up a large salad bowl. "Hungry?"

There was a small grin on her face, though I could tell it was forced. Still, she seemed to be in a much better mood now that she had been earlier in the day, when I woke up to her phone call in a Salina Cruz motel.

First we got high, then we ate. Not much was said during either activity. Afterwards we sat out on my back patio, listening to the waves breaking in the distance. It was a cool night with a gentle breeze. I tilted my head back and looked up at the sky, dark and clear, thousands of stars scattered about. Would I be able to see any of them from my jail cell? Probably not. A part of me knew I should have been thinking up a plan better than simply "deny all involvement," but I also just wanted to sit there and stare up at the stars. Enjoy the moment, take it all in.

So that's what I did. Instead of calling the embassy, driving to Nica, or buying a plane ticket to Chicago, I just sat there with Kerstin, stoned to the gills, looking up at the nighttime sky.

☼

She was lying on her stomach, face turned away, sheet pulled down to just below her waist. I lay there beside her, mind still cloudy from the night before. Eventually—five minutes later, a half-hour, I don't know—she turned her head and looked over at me. I could tell by her eyes that she'd been awake for some time.

"I want you to know," she said, rolling on to her back, staring up at the ceiling. "It's not a good thing. What you did, I mean."

For the next few minutes the only sounds in the room came from the fan, which desperately needed some WD-40. My brain wasn't in peak operating condition, but I did manage to develop a theory while lying there: after our phone call yesterday morning, Kerstin went to visit Mateo's wife, Yolanda. Maybe it was just to follow-up and let Yolanda know that her husband's coconspirator was on his way back to town. And maybe that's when Yolanda decided to let Kerstin in on her / my / our secret.

"But I can understand why you felt like you had to do something. For Javy and the girls." She turned her head and looked over at me. "It *was* an accident, right?" she asked, eyes pleading with me. She needed to know that the man with whom she'd had a quasi-relationship for the past two years wasn't a murderer—or, at the very least, that he wasn't a premeditated one.

"Of course," I said, figuring there was no point in denying anymore. "I thought I'd be able to get them to confess. I wanted to record them on my phone and then turn it over to Gilberto." I didn't add that yes, in hindsight, I could see how fucking stupid this plan was. "I wish I'd gone about it differently. I wish I would've done *everything* differently: not loaded the gun, not gotten Mateo involved. Just thinking about Yolanda and the kids… it's… I don't know…"

"What are you going to do?"

This answer came easy: "I have no idea. Absolutely none."

☼

After Kerstin left to go teach a morning yoga class, I put a couple of frozen waffles into a microwave that didn't so much heat things up as it sped up the thawing process. After topping them with a large, unhealthy amount of syrup, I took advantage of the ensuing sugar buzz, grabbing my longboard and heading down to the beach. Waves weren't great, but there was a little something to be had. I paddled out and joined a lineup consisting of just two other guys, neither of whom I recognized, speaking a language I couldn't discern (Dutch? Danish? German?). They were terrible surfers but understood lineup etiquette, which is preferable to the opposite combination. After a half-hour of them letting me have free reign over every set, I started deferring to them, yelling *go go go, paddle paddle paddle, arriba arriba*. It was a fifty-fifty proposition whether they'd catch any given wave. They laughed when they didn't, and also when they did. Vibes were good.

But all good things come to an end. At one point I glanced towards the beach and saw someone waving out at me, and the only person in Oaxaca who could produce this particular silhouette was Gilberto Jiménez. What made the visual all the more troubling were the couple of guys standing beside him, one on each side, dressed in all green.

For a brief moment I considered paddling out into the Pacific, testing my luck and hoping I'd cross paths with a fishing boat before a shark spotted me. A few sets passed underneath me before I tried for another wave. When I finally did paddle for one, I was so rattled by the sight of Gilberto that I ended up pearling on the goddamn thing, which is almost impossible to do when you're in waist-high peelers on a longboard. It was some straight up kook shit. After a brief underwater rinsing I wished was longer, I climbed back onto my board and paddled to shore. What a perfect way to end to my surfing "career."

Once I got to shore, Gilberto didn't come meet me halfway. Of course not. He just stayed where he was, standing underneath the shade of a tree. I wondered if I walked away from him, down the beach, whether he'd even try to come after me. Most likely not, which was probably why he'd brought along the two other guys. I closed my eyes and took a deep breath, forcing myself to accept the inevitability of the current situation. Once I got close enough to realize that the two sidekicks looked like a couple of prepubescent teenagers, I was able to relax some. At least they weren't federales.

"Buenos días," I said, trying to seem relaxed. *"¿Qué tal?"*

Gilberto ignored the lame greeting and got right to it: "I'm going to need you to come down to the station."

"Can I take my board home first?"

"Hazlo rápido."

The two sidekicks followed me back to my house. (Gilberto didn't want the extra steps; he went right back to the station.) I put my board in the shed, threw on a t-shirt, and grabbed my White Sox hat. Before heading back outside, I opened the fridge and pulled out three Pacíficos. I offered one to each of my chaperones. They both seemed tempted but ultimately turned down the offer. We started walking.

I'd been actively avoiding my new reality for the past couple of days. I knew this. Instead of reaching out to anyone for advice, I was getting drunk and stoned. I was surfing. I was drinking a few beers on the walk over to the police station, for what was sure to be the one of the most important conversations of my life. Some might even be tempted to call this self-sabotage, but what was the alternative? Confronting the issues head-on? Actually dealing with something? I laughed out loud at the thought, startling the two kids walking beside me.

NINE

I finished all three beers in the ten-minute walk to the station. A fourth would have been nice. Despite the moderate buzz, my stomach dropped when I saw the slew of police vehicles parked outside of the station. Particularly nauseating was the black SUV with *Policía Federal* written on its side.

Inside the station was *the* nightmare scenario: instead of a multigenerational contingent of SoCal bros waiting for me in the lobby, some federales were now standing around. Boots shined, pants pressed, god fucking help me. One of my two teenage chaperones directed me back to Gilberto's office, where I found him sitting at his desk, looking fat and uncomfortable, though not just in the normal, physical sense. He was anxious and uneasy, much like myself. This was likely due to the federale sitting across from him, in one of the two chairs that had been cleared of debris in the past twenty-four hours. The federale stood up and offered his hand. It was the same guy I'd seen from a distance a few days ago.

"Juan Martín Rodriguez. *Policía Federal Ministerial.*"

About fifty, give or take, he was the exact opposite of Gilberto in terms of physical appearance: tall, lean, well put together. His tight buzz cut was a mixture of black and gray, and his hairline, like that of most Latinos, hadn't changed since he was sixteen.

"Tony," I said, reaching for his hand, and in the handshake that ensued, he nearly broke mine.

"Have a seat, Tony," he said, in accented but good English. "Spanish or English?"

"*No importa.*"

He continued in Spanish: "I want to be clear: this isn't an interrogation. It's a conversation. It's an opportunity for you to help us figure out what happened to Travis McBride. You're aware of his disappearance, correct?"

"Of course."

"And you're also aware that we have two eyewitnesses saying that you shot him in the head, execution-style?"

I felt a small urge to jump in and correct him on a few things. One, it was *Square Face* who caused the gun to go off. Two, it was an *accident*. Three, the bullet had gone into Travis's *neck*, not his head. And four, it wasn't even, like, the *middle* of his neck—it was more like a grazing.

"¿Señor Winslow?"

"I wasn't aware of… their account of events," I said, trying my best to come off as relaxed, even though my heart was racing and it felt like if I looked down, there'd be a puddle of sweat on the floor. "I don't know why they'd be saying that. I didn't have anything to do with whatever happened."

"If you have any information—anything at all—I urge you to share it now. Because we *will* find out what happened, *¿me entiendes?*"

"I hope you do."

I glanced over at Gilberto, who still looked every bit as uncomfortable as when I'd first walked in. The pay-for-play was over for him, at least for a little while. No more side income streams. The federales' presence had put an end to that, but could they also be investigating some of *his* past misdeeds? *Pretty nice house you got there, Gilberto. Mind if we look into your financials?* I didn't know what to think here, and judging by the look on Gilberto's face and the amount of sweat that had soaked through his uniform, neither did he.

"Now," said Juan Martín. "Let's have that conversation."

"I thought we just did."

He smiled. "That was just an introduction. Sit down, Tony."

The questions came quickly, which was a good thing for me. Gave me less time to think, to second-guess myself. I was surprised by how well I responded, how easily the lies came. Maybe the beers really had been a good idea.

No, I hadn't been hiding on the side of the road, waiting for Mateo to deliver the three guys to me. (This, of course, wasn't a lie, and in hindsight it made more sense than me riding along in the back of the van.)

Yes, I was with Javy the night he got into an argument with three guys at La Hija's. But that was the extent of my involvement.

Yes, I'm sure.

Positive.

Sure, yeah, I'd heard some rumors that the guys had been involved in some sexual assaults. Everyone in Punta Cita had heard those.

No, I didn't know who the victims were.

No clue.

Juan Martín looked at me for a long time after this one. "*¿Estás seguro?*"

"*Claro.*"

"You think you have a drinking problem, Tony?"

"With alcohol?"

He just looked at me, like: *No, asshole, with kombucha.*

"Sometimes I drink a little too much, but who doesn't?"

"I don't. Lots of people don't."

"Sometimes, yeah, I do," I shrugged. "But I don't get why that's relevant here."

"*¿Mexico, verdad*? Anything goes, right? You can just do whatever you want down here, *no hay problema, ¿sí o no*?"

"Jesus. How'd you get there? You asked me about drinking, not—"

"*¿Sí o no*?"

"That's not at all what I think."

"No?"

"But maybe some other people do."

"Gringos?"

"Yeah, sure, but I'm not your typical gringo."

He laughed as he got up from his chair. "Every gringo says that."

Gilberto also stood up. It was the fastest I'd ever seen him move. I did the same.

"You don't have any travel plans coming up, do you?" said Juan Martín, though it felt more like an order than a question.

"Not that I… no, I don't."

"*Qué bueno*," he said. "We'll talk again soon, okay?"

"Sure, yeah," I said, afraid to ask a follow-up such as: *Um, why?*

Walking back to my place, it seemed like everyone's eyes settled on me for a moment too long. Was this a new form of social anxiety I'd suddenly developed? Or were people really staring at me? It wasn't until I was unlocking my front gate that I realized the two teenage deputies were twenty feet behind me.

"¿Me siguieron?"

They laughed. Of course they'd followed me.

I headed inside while they remained out at the gate, making sure, presumably, that I wouldn't be going anywhere. This may have technically been a violation of my rights, due process—something, I'm sure—but I figured I had more important things to worry about.

☼

Other than the occasional text or e-mail, my sister and I didn't talk a whole lot. It wasn't that we had a bad relationship; we'd just grown up and pursued two distinct lifestyles. I was a degenerate, and Sarah was a normal, functioning adult with a job and health insurance.

After listening to shitty hold music for a few minutes: "Tony?"

"I think you need some new music."

"For what?"

"For people on hold."

"Yeah, well, the good stuff costs more."

"But how many potential clients have hung up after thirty seconds of listening to that shit? Might be worth the investment."

"I don't put important people on hold."

"Fair."

"What's up? You okay?"

"Yeah, yeah, I'm fine," I said, because that's just what you say. "How are things in Chicago?"

"Same old. I lead a much more boring life than you."

"You might be surprised."

"I doubt it," she said, and then: "What's going on? I know this isn't just a random check-in."

I took a pull from my Pacífico. "I need a little legal advice."

"Oh, Jesus. What happened?"

"It's a bit complicated."

"It always is," she said. "Down there or up here?"

"Down here."

"Let's hear it."

I gave her an overview of the situation—not everything, of course, but enough for her to have a rough idea about what was going on. Left out of this synopsis, however, was even the slightest hint of my own involvement. This wasn't my intention when I picked up the phone and made the call, but the words just never came. *Oh yeah, I was there and, ha-ha, it's a funny story, but actually I, uh, kind of shot the kid in the neck.* Instead, I told her my reason for calling was that I wanted to help Mateo, that I wanted to know what *his* legal options looked like. My hope here was that I'd not only be able to help him, but I'd also be able to apply the legal advice to my own situation.

The first thing she said after I was through: "Jesus Christ, Tony."

Second thing: "He'd need to talk with a lawyer in Mexico. You do know it's this whole other country, right? With a whole different legal system?"

"Is that right?"

"The spare tire thing is pretty damning. And such an obvious lie would then reasonably cast doubt over everything else he says," she said. "What makes you believe him?"

"I just— I know he wasn't involved, not in the way they're saying he is."

"But his story makes no sense."

"He's not at fault here. I just know that."

A brief pause, then the natural follow-up: "Are *you* involved somehow?"

"No," I said, maybe too quickly. "He's just a good friend of mine. I want to help him out."

More silence. Sarah was too smart for my bullshit, and even though we didn't talk much, she was still my sister. She knew me. Now it was just a matter of whether she'd call me out or let me be.

"I'll ask an old colleague from Mexico City. I think he did some work down there, so he might be able to offer something. But still, I can't guarantee it'll be anything useful."

"Anything at all would be helpful."

"I'll get back to you in the next couple of days. That okay?"

"Perfect," I said, wondering if she'd have to call a Mexican jail in order to talk to me at that point. "How're the kids doing?

"Tess is good, set to graduate this year. Then it's off to law school, despite all my warnings."

"Always wanted to be like her mom."

"Terrifying."

"I know."

"And Dylan's apparently thinking about dropping out after a year. Or as he likes to put it: take a gap year."

"Obama's daughter did that, right?"

"Yeah, but that was right after high school, and she went to Harvard. He's already at Illinois. All you have to do is show up."

"Yeah, but you also have to live in Urbana-Champaign for four years."

"Fair point."

"What's he want to do during the gap year?"

"Says he wants to travel and 'experience life,' whatever the hell that means."

"I can empathize."

"That's what worries me."

I laughed.

"I'm kidding," she said, though she definitely wasn't. "Listen, I have to take another call."

"Billable hours?"

"Everything's billable."

"Even this?"

"Except this. I'll be in touch, okay?"

"I owe you."

"No, you don't."

After hanging up, I walked into the kitchen and grabbed another beer. I sat down at the kitchen table and stared at the splattered grease above my stove. I couldn't remember the last time I'd cleaned it, or if I ever had.

☼

She called back an hour later. I though this quicker-than-expected turnaround might be a good sign.

It was not.

"Hey, that was—"

"What the hell's going on down there?"

"What do you mean?"

"You haven't seen the news?"

My stomach dropped. "What news?"

"Do you not have the internet?"

"I'm living in Mexico, not the year 1900."

"Check out Rox News."

"Why would I ever do that?"

"Fair question, but Carrie Owens has an interview up with some guy named... Kevin McBride? I'm reading it right now."

"She's down here? In Punta Cita?"

"Apparently."

As I waited for my prehistoric laptop to get going, I briefly considered an alternative: throwing it against a wall. Another option: repeatedly smashing it with the cast iron skillet I kept over on the stove.

"You know," Sarah said, interrupting these deep, meaningful thoughts, "whatever normally happens in cases like this probably doesn't apply anymore."

"What do you mean?"

"Not only was an American murdered—or, allegedly murdered—but now there's media attention. Safe to say they'll want this wrapped up quickly."

I'd heard the same line from Gilberto, so this wasn't exactly news. But now that the very worst elements of the American media apparatus were involved, things could only get worse.

"The good thing is that if your friend really is innocent, the investigation should clear him."

"Yeah— that's— yeah, that's good."

"But if it drags out and the media stays down there, that's not a good look for the town, or the Mexican tourism industry as a whole. So if they can't wrap it up legitimately, they might charge someone just to relieve the pressure. That shit happens up here all the time, too."

"Christ…"

"I'm still waiting to hear back from my friend. He might get more interested after I forward him this, so stay tuned. And Tony?"

"Yeah?"

"I have to ask, as both a lawyer and your sister, is there anything you're not telling me?"

"No, I swear," I said, too quickly again. "Mateo's just been a really good friend, and I know he can't afford a lawyer. So… yeah, I mean, that's pretty much it."

"You sure?"

"I'd tell you if it wasn't."

A brief pause. "Okay. I'll talk to you soon."

"Thanks again."

Once my laptop finally became functional, I opened a browser and did something I never thought

I'd do: I went to RoxNews.com. I had to scroll for a while, but it didn't take long to find the interview. Sandwiched between a couple headlines blaming immigrants for all of the United States' woes, I found this one: *Family seeks answers after disappearance in Mexico.*

TEN

"I'm here in Punta Cita, Mexico, where a dream vacation..." said Carrie Owens, standing in front of La Vista del Mar, microphone in hand, "...turned into a nightmare."

Carrie was a younger and slightly more annoying version of Nancy Grace (yes, somehow: *more* annoying). She didn't have her own show yet, but given all the misleading hyperbole that flowed so naturally out of her mouth, it wouldn't be long until she had an hour-long time slot. After that highly original opening line, she went on to cover the basics: two brothers and a lifelong friend; vacation in Mexico; stopped on their way to the airport; ordered into the woods, down onto their knees; one was "executed"; two managed to escape; the body had yet to be found.

The camera then panned to a man standing beside her.

"I only want two things," said a somber-looking Kevin McBride. "To get justice for my son, and to bring him home."

The video cut next to a stern-faced Brody, who was apparently doing his best impression of… an annoyed Mark Wahlberg? Then it was Chad's turn. The kid was hopelessly pitiful.

Back to Carrie. "Kevin, you mentioned something about an unfounded rumor spreading about the boys. Can you tell us a little more about that?"

Boys? They're in their goddamn twenties.

"We think this might be a case of misplaced vigilante justice."

"How so?"

"To justify my son's murder, someone started the rumor that the boys were involved in a sexual assault—"

"Which isn't true?"

"It's absolutely false," he said, confident, indignant. I hated this man. "It's just a rumor started by someone desperate to draw attention away from what he did to my son."

"Was a sexual assault ever reported?"

"No," he said, staring directly into the camera now. He had this incredulous look on his face, like he couldn't believe he had to respond to such baseless speculation. "And the women who were rumored to be involved not only didn't report anything, they're not even in town anymore. None of it makes any sense."

The women rumored to be involved? Not in town? What the hell does that mean?

"Are you saying they might have been involved in some sort of smear campaign?"

"I'm not saying whether they are or they're not. I'm just saying things aren't adding up."

I wanted to puke, and also kill him (not literally, but also not *not* literally; I was somewhere in between).

"There had recently been another death in Punta Cita, correct?"

"There was, yes. Tragically."

"A local by the name of... Javy Rodriguez," said Carrie, reading from a card, Javy so insignificant that she couldn't be bothered to memorize his name. "And another rumor that's been spreading around town—and I'm sorry to bring this up, but I need to give our viewers an idea of what you're dealing with—is that your sons and their friend were involved in Mr. Rodriguez's death."

Kevin looked away from the camera, shaking his head. This was his go-to move. "It's crazy, what they're trying to do here. Yes, Mr. Rodriguez died, which is very sad—it's tragic—and I send my sincerest condolences to his family. But his death was ruled an accident by the medical examiner. What more needs to be said?"

"It must be terrible, dealing with all this, when all you want is to find Travis," Carrie said, Javy already an afterthought.

"It's been tough," said Kevin, acting like he was somehow the biggest victim in all of this. "But we *will* get justice for my son."

☼

I stared at my laptop for a long time after the video stopped playing. Since when had Javy's death been ruled an accident? Or was Kevin McBride just getting out ahead of the story and putting his spin on things? And what he said about the women, it made no sense. How would he know if they'd left town or not? And if they had left town… like, *why?*

I stood up, started pacing around my kitchen. There was a small radio on the counter I hadn't used in years. I picked it up with every intention of immediately then spiking it into the ground, but then another idea came to me: I turned it on, volume all the way up. I found something with a nice reggae beat, something the two teenage chaperones outside might enjoy. Then I walked out back, climbed onto my shed, and jumped over the fence. It felt like my knees might explode upon landing, but I managed to stay upright.

Marysol's fruit stand was in the same spot every day, in this little plaza in the middle of town. But today it wasn't. Far as I could tell, it wasn't anywhere.

Staying as far away from Calle Dorado as I could manage, I made my way over to La Vista del Mar. I walked through the lobby and up to the second floor, just another gringo tourist returning to his room. I asked the first maid I came across if she'd seen Luisa.

"Hoy no está aqui."

"Was she supposed to work today?"

"No sé."

I got the same answers from maids on the third and fourth floors.

I left the resort and creeped my way back through town, until I came to a well-traveled dirt road used exclusively by locals. A quarter-mile later I was in a neighborhood made up of small homes constructed with some combination of concrete, adobe, and aluminum. Most of them were right along the road, directly beside one another, though a few others (typically the larger ones) had yards out in front of them. There weren't any shops or restaurants around, save for a little store run out of one family's home.

I waved at some people I recognized, a few I didn't. Some were just sitting around, shooting the shit, while others were working, doing this and that—fixing a bike, hanging laundry, sweeping a floor. Eventually I came to a small adobe house with a thick wooden door. The windows on each of its four sides had bars, not glass. I knocked on the door and waited.

Nothing.

Knocked again.

Still: nothing.

I walked around back, tried that door.

No response.

I looked through the back window: no lights, no movement. No one was home.

I walked out front and asked one of their neighbors, this middle-aged man in a Real Madrid jersey who'd been watching my every move (understandably so), *"¿Conoce usted a Marysol y Paloma?"*

"Sí, claro."

"Do you know where they are?"

"Probably working. They run a fruit stand."

"Do you know where it's at today?"

"The plaza, usually. I don't know if they go anywhere else."

"That's what I thought, but they weren't there."

He shrugged. "There's a maid who lives there too."

"Luisa?"

"*Sí*. Luisa."

The man's wife appeared in the doorway. "Luisa," she said. "She works at La Vista del Mar."

"I just checked, she wasn't there."

She shrugged. *"Pues, no sé."*

I thanked them and started jogging back towards town. Heart beating a mile a minute, one solitary thought bouncing around in my head: *What the fuck?*

I stopped a minute later, once I realized I didn't know where I was going or what I should do next. I was also pretty out of shape. I'd make a pit stop at Vicente's. I'd relax, regroup, figure something out. I also really needed a drink.

☼

"No las he visto," said Vicente, after I asked if he'd seen the three women. "Which is strange, because I do usually see them when they're heading to work in the morning."

"But you didn't today?"

"Sometimes I'm making coffee, doing something around the house." He lived in a small house directly beside the bar, though the boundary between the two wasn't entirely clear to me. "So I guess I don't always see them."

"How about last night?" I asked, full-on fucking panicking at this point.

He closed his eyes for a brief moment, trying to remember. "No, I don't… yeah, I don't think I did."

"God damn it."

"Tony," he said, voice lower now. "This have something to do with Mateo?"

"Maybe— probably— *fuck*. I saw them yesterday. Marysol and Paloma, anyway. They were working, it was normal, but now— Jesus— I don't know…" I stood up, put some pesos on the bar. *"Gracias."*

"Ten cuidado, joven."

In most circumstances, it was some good advice: *Be careful.*

But right now I wasn't so sure.

☼

First thing I'd do: find them.

Second thing: convince them to report the assaults to the police.

Yes. Easy.

The kidnapping and accessory to murder charges facing Mateo would immediately then get dropped. I could envision him calmly walking out of his jail cell afterwards, everyone agreeing—Rox News, los federales, the pope; fucking *everyone*—that some vigilante justice had indeed been warranted on this particular occasion.

It was the best-case scenario.

It was also fucking delusional.

I had no idea—none—where the women were. Sure, there *was* the possibility that they'd left on their own accord, but the way the elder McBride had so confidently proclaimed that "the women rumored to be involved were no longer in town" had me concerned. Could he have paid them off? I found myself hoping that this *had* been the case, even though I couldn't imagine Marysol accepting money in return for their silence. It just didn't fit with what I knew about her, though it wasn't like we were lifelong friends or anything. If something like that had taken place—an offer was made—I wondered how Kevin would have reacted if they'd refused to take his money. Would he have tried to keep them quiet some other way?

I was almost back to my place (after the brief pit stop at Vicente's) when Walt Hereford came rushing up to me. Of all the people to keep running into, he was both my best and worst option.

"Tony, Tony!" he called out, and then, stepping closer, lowering his voice: "There are some rumors."

"About what?"

"About you."

"Oh, yeah?"

"That you might be involved in all this…" he said, staring at me through his oversized aviators. With a bucket hat on top of his head, he looked like an overweight Gilligan trying to pass himself off as Maverick from *Top Gun*. "No way, right?"

"The fuck you think?" I forced out some laughter and walked past him.

"If you need anything," he called out, "you know where to find me."

After climbing over my fence and onto my shed, I snuck back into my house. If circumstances had been different I might have found this a bit unsettling, just how easy it was to break into my own house. I turned the volume down on the radio and opened my laptop. No updates from Rox News. Nothing in my inbox from Sarah. I typed "Mexican legal system" into Google and started browsing through the 94,500,000 results. Nothing seemed particularly useful, not that I really had any chance of interpreting the legalese staring back at me.

A knock on the front door saved me from a dense block of text averaging two footnotes per sentence. Up until a week ago, the only person who regularly stopped by my house was Kerstin, and though there were occasional visits from a few of my neighbors, I mostly didn't have to worry about unexpected visitors. This clearly wasn't the case anymore.

I stood up and started towards the front door, mind racing ahead of me. Juan Martín would be outside. He'd tell me that Mateo confessed. They found the body. They found the gun. He'd smirk and tell me that I'm a fucking idiot. This was my fate. I knew it.

Not wanting the reality to set in any sooner than it had to, I didn't bother looking out the front window. Hand on the doorknob, I wondered what my cellmates would be like, what kind of face tattoos they'd have.

It wasn't Juan Martín.

And my two sentries had apparently taken a break.

It was Kevin McBride. "We need to talk."

"Sure," I said, after a moment. I stepped aside, holding open the door.

He walked inside, all the way into the kitchen. *Come on in, dude! Make yourself at home!* I followed him there, where we both remained standing, kitchen table between us.

"I know you killed my son," he said, getting right to it. "You should be in fucking jail right now."

"Listen, I don't know—"

"They're going to figure it out eventually. You know that, right? Whether the driver gives you up or we find my son's body, it's going to happen."

I shrugged, holding out my hands. "I don't know what you're talking about."

"That's really how you're going to play this, huh?"

"I'm sorry for your loss— I am— but you can't just go around throwing out accusations like this."

"Oh, fuck off. Do yourself a favor and get this shit over with. Let there be some goddamn justice in this world for once."

"*Justice*? You really want to talk about justice? What about Javy?"

"My boys didn't have anything to do with that."

There it was—*boys* again. "Classified as an accidental death? How'd you pull that one off?"

"I had nothing to do with that. I'm not employed by the coroner's office in Oaxaca."

"No, but you're a rich, entitled gringo."

"And you're not?"

I laughed. "I'm not rich."

"Clearly," he said with a snicker, gesturing around at my casita. Even now, during a conversation that centered around the death of his son, the guy was incapable of letting an opportunity pass in which he could point out his economic superiority. "But you probably have enough to fill a few pockets, anyway."

I wondered where the line was, between what he actually knew and what he was pretending to know. If Gilberto ever got busted, I wouldn't be far behind him, and the thought of ending up in a cell with his fat ass—remote as that possibility might have been—was *the* nightmare scenario. The heavy breathing, the sweating, the flatulence.

"What about the women you mentioned?" I said. "During your interview with Carrie Owens."

"Who?"

"The women who 'left town,' according to you."

"That's just what I heard," he said, little grin on his face now.

"The fuck did you do to them?"

The grin widened.

Jesus Christ. The bastard was enjoying this.

"Let me a steal a line from you," he said, "and just say that I don't know what you're talking about."

"Motherfucker…" I threw a chair aside and circled the table. Grabbed him by his shirt. "Where are they?"

"Get your hands—"

I pushed him against the wall. A cheap watercolor of an old fisherman fell to the ground. Right next to it was the rosary Marysol had given me. I wondered if I might be able to strangle the guy with it. "Where are they?"

"Maybe they went back to Guatemala."

"I swear, if you did anything to them…"

"What? What're you gonna do? Kill me, too?"

I let go of his shirt, took a few steps back. I needed to calm down. Otherwise I might prove him right.

"This is pretty simple," he said, straightening out his shirt. "You own up to what you did, let me take my son home. My guess is that if you do that, those women will start selling sliced pineapples again. Call it a hunch. And you should be thanking me, anyway."

"For what?"

"For not giving Carrie Owens your name."

"Yeah, why didn't you?"

"So we could have this conversation." He smiled. "And so you could enjoy your last day or two as a free man, before the world finds out that you're a murderer."

"You preferred putting pressure on me by kidnapping innocent women? As opposed to just letting the media come after me?"

He shrugged. "Without the women, what's your incentive to confess?"

"You're an *evil* motherfucker."

"What's that make you then?"

"I didn't..." I said, vision blurring, pressure building in my head. "I didn't..." A migraine was coming. Soon. *Now*. I pointed towards the front door. "Get out of my house."

"How many lives are you willing to trade for your own freedom? What's the phrase for that kind of thing? Gringo entitlement?"

"Get *the fuck* out of my house!"

He walked out without shutting the door. I stumbled my way into the living room and collapsed onto the couch. I closed my eyes and rubbed the sides of my head. My thoughts were jumbled and incoherent, save for one: the pistol I'd buried out in the woods, and how easy it'd be to drive out there, dig it up. Wasn't far. Then I'd point it at Kevin's face, until he told me what he did to Marysol and the two girls.

Another option: digging it up and pressing it against the side of my own head. Yeah. That'd be another way to relieve the pressure.

ELEVEN

Still on the couch, first hints of morning light coming through the windows, a plan beginning to take shape in my mind: I'd go to the police station and confess, and then for the next twenty years I'd spend my days reading novels, doing pushups, and trying not to get killed. I'd get paroled around sixty-five and move to a small town, one without any tourists or expats running around. I'd buy an old RV, park it under a tree, and spend the rest of my years as a recluse.

I stood up, put on a clean shirt, and walked to Kerstin's. No coffee, no breakfast. No final surf session. I didn't want to linger. Didn't want to give myself an opportunity to second guess what I was doing.

She was sitting outside: drinking tea, reading.

"Hey," she said, glancing up, and then: "What's wrong? What happened?"

I'd never been any good at poker. "I have to… well, uh…"

She stood up, walked towards me. "What?"

"Go to the police, tell them what happened. What I did."

She shook her head. "What? No, just— *no*— you can't just walk in there and confess and expect everything to be okay, that's not how—"

"It's the only way."

"Only way to what?"

"To help Mateo. He shouldn't have to take the fall for this. It was my idea. Everything was my idea."

"But it's not like he's off the hook once you go in. If anything, that just confirms he's lying."

She was right, of course, but this would only happen if I told the cops the *entire* truth. I wasn't going to do that. I was going to say that I'd tricked Mateo, that he had no idea what I'd been planning with the whole flat tire scheme. He might've been an idiot, but he wasn't a criminal. He'd kept quiet and stuck to the flat tire story because it was *me* who had threatened him. My confession wouldn't just help Mateo, but it'd also allow the three women to come back from wherever it was they'd been taken. I'd go to jail, and that'd be that.

"I have to at least try," I said. "I'm out of options at this point."

We stood there for a while, half-hugging, half not, mumbling words and then repeating them. *Are you sure? Yes. Really? I don't know. Okay? Okay.* I left before either of us had the chance to say anything meaningful.

I hadn't planned on making any additional stops prior to the police station, but a few minutes later I found myself walking towards Mateo's house.

"*Buenos días,*" I said to the anxious kids roaming around outside. "*¿Dónde está tu mamá?*"

A couple of the younger ones ran inside. "*¡Mamá!*"

Yolanda walked outside a moment later, wiping her hands on an apron. It looked like she hadn't slept in days. She told her kids to get outside, and to stay there. Then to me: "*Venga, venga.*"

I walked inside, sat down at a small table in the kitchen. She handed me a small plate with some pan dulce. "*¿Algo pasó?*" she asked, sitting down across from me. "*¿Qué?*"

"I'm turning myself in," I said, staring down at the plate. "It's the only way I can help Mateo at this point."

"*¿Qué?*"

"I'm turning myself in."

"*No. No puedes.*"

When I finally glanced up at her, I was surprised to see a look of sheer terror on her face. Not gratitude, not reluctant acceptance. Not even confusion—just pure fucking *terror*.

"You can't," she said again, shaking her head.

"I'll tell them I tricked Mateo, that he had nothing to do with this."

"Tony, please, you have to—"

"I got him into this, Yolanda. It's only right. If anyone deserves to be in jail, it's me."

"What those men did was evil, with the girls and then to Javy. Mateo wanted to help."

"If the cops find out everything that actually happened, we're both screwed, him *and* me. Unless I get out ahead of it, and why should both of us end up jail?"

I didn't mention that Marysol and the two girls had been kidnapped, and how that was another reason I was turning myself in. Why give the poor woman even more to worry about?

"Tony, this doesn't make sense—"

"I don't have kids. I don't have a family I need to support. And I'm an American, so I'll get treated differently."

"You can't—"

"This was my idea, not his," I said. "That's what it comes down to."

"*No hay cuerpo*," she said, shaking her head. "And without a body, they can only hold him for so long."

"You sure about that?"

She ignored the question. "Do you think they're really going to believe you? That you just 'tricked' my husband? That he's that stupid?"

"I'll say I threatened his family."

"Dios mío..."

We went back and forth for a while. She grew increasingly annoyed with me, saying a few things in Spanish I couldn't quite understand. Probably for the best. Eventually I broke down and told her about Marysol and the girls, and how I was fairly certain they'd been kidnapped. She seemed dumbfounded by this revelation, asking me to repeat myself. I did, and then I also told her what Kevin McBride had said. I was thinking this would be the end of the argument. The women's lives were on the line. There was no other option.

But she just looked at me like I was an idiot. "You think he's just going to *let* them go once you turn yourself in? You honestly think that's going to happen?"

"Why wouldn't he?"

"Do you even know where they are? Or if they're still alive?"

"No, but—"

She stood up, started pacing. "What's his incentive to let them go? Kidnapping is a crime, isn't it? So once they're free, they could just report the kidnapping along with the sexual assaults."

"Yeah, but…" This was a good point, one I hadn't considered.

"Jesus, Tony. You need to find these women. That's your only hope. That's Mateo's only hope."

"But… how do I find them?" I asked after a moment, because she seemed to have an answer for pretty much everything else.

"*No sé*. But there's a way. There's always a way."

She gave me some more pan dulce then told me to get the hell out of her house, go figure something out. In terms of my own self-interest, it was a pretty good turn of events (to put it mildly): maybe I wouldn't end up in jail for the next twenty years. But how was I supposed to go about finding the kidnapped women?

I didn't have any idea until I got back to Calle Dorado and saw two old men walking with fishing poles. Then I did.

☼

There's a makeshift bay at one end of town, formed by a couple of jetties jutting out into the ocean. I knew Walt would be out there on his 25′ *Natalya,* a boat named after his wife, who, according to local gossip, was of the mail-order variety. This was easily confirmed by the eye test: there was no way—fucking *none*—that someone as attractive as her would ever end up with someone like Walt Hereford.

But he'd apparently become too much to bear for her, and just a few weeks ago she'd moved back to eastern Siberia. What she was saying, basically, was that life in subzero temperatures was preferable to living anywhere in the world—tropical paradise included—with Walt Hereford. I found this reasonable.

"Hey, Walt," I called out as I approached. He was standing towards the back of the boat, and whatever he was doing seemed to involve about a half-mile of rope. "What's up, man?"

He spun around at the sound of my voice, nearly tripping over the rope at his feet. "Tony?"

"You got any charters today?"

He seemed nervous, which in turn made *me* grow somewhat nervous. Maybe he was just surprised to see me? After four years of living in Punta Cita, I'd never once sought him out, never once initiated a conversation with the man. And now here I was.

"Yeah, I got a group this morning," he said. "In about an hour."

"Can you cancel on them?"

"What?"

"I actually *need* you to cancel on them."

"What do you— why would I do that?"

"You mind if I get on?"

"The boat?"

"Yes, Walt," I said. "The fucking boat."

Once aboard I took off my sunglasses and walked towards him, until there was only about a foot between us. I told him what I wanted to do.

"Jesus Christ, Tony."

"Yeah."

"You really think that's the best way to handle this?"

"Unless you have a better idea, in which case I'm all ears."

After a moment, he said, "Are you sure they did it?"

"I was there."

This caught him by surprise. "You saw them kill Javy?"

"No, but I saw one of them sexually assaulting somebody. I think it's pretty easy to connect the dots after that."

"But didn't they rule Javy's death an accident?"

"You know that's bullshit."

He looked away from me, out over the water. I was asking a lot of him.

"I guess this will be my down south moment, eh?" he said.

There's a stupid cliché among expats that you aren't fully assimilated until you do something so crazy that your pre-Mexico self wouldn't recognize the person you've become. Just as much bad shit happens north of the border, but expats love clichés more than anything in the world (including this one: romanticizing their sepia-toned lives in Mexico to friends back home).

"Is that a yes?"

He held out his hand. "Fuckin' A."

We shook. Maybe Walt wasn't so bad after all.

Or maybe it's just that I was.

☼

After explaining my change of plans to Kerstin (I could tell she'd been crying since our earlier conversation, and I'm not proud to admit how good this made me feel), I asked if she could do me a small favor.

"That's not a small favor."

I'd even left out quite a few details, including those related to what would happen after she did her part. "Medium-sized?"

"What makes you think they'll even go for this?"

"Don't change."

"What?"

"Just wear what you're wearing right now."

Black yoga pants, black sports bra.

She shook her head. "You're all the same."

☼

It wasn't hard to find. Three rocks, still right there, just beside the tree. I moved them aside, dug my fingers into the dirt, and pulled out the plastic bag.

Steel against tailbone, uncomfortable but not foreign, I wondered if this was just who I was now, the kind of guy who walks around with a gun tucked into his waistband.

☼

Back at my place, I told myself that for once in my life I needed to be sober and clear-headed. No shots of tequila, no one-hitters. Nothing up my nose.

I refreshed RoxNews.com about a hundred times (the problem with being sober and clear-headed: anxiety) but didn't see any updates on the "Nightmare in Mexico." I also refreshed my inbox constantly (even though it updated automatically), so it was probably just a couple seconds after Sarah hit 'send' up in Chicago that I saw a message with the following subject line: *Just in case you find yourself accused of anything…*

In the message itself she explained that "under no fucking circumstances" should I answer any questions. In fact, besides asking the interviewer (interrogator?) to call the embassy on my behalf, I wasn't to speak at all. "Not a fucking word" was her exact phrasing.

I didn't respond to the email, choosing instead to turn up Pearl Jam's "Given to Fly" and grab a beer from the fridge. The change in thinking with regard to the booze wasn't just due to my impulsivity and weakness (partially, yes, of course it was), but also because I figured the longer I waited around, the more nervous I'd get, and that a beer or two might actually do me some good. (I believe the technical term here is "rationalization.")

The call—finally, dear Christ—came during my third beer.

"How'd it go?"

"They'll be out there at noon."

"Was it hard?"

"Not really," said Kerstin. "I just said it'd be a good way to relax, get their mind off things."

"That's it?"

"And that afterwards they could try out some yoga."

"Thank you. I owe you."

"Just don't screw this up, okay?"

"Of course," I said, chuckling to myself after I hung up, because *of course* I was going to screw this up. It was just a matter of to what extent.

After finishing off the rest of my beer, I glanced out in front of my house, where once again I discovered that I had two sentries standing guard. Intermittent surveillance was certainly a unique strategy. I turned the radio up and got ready to head out through the back: keys, phone, wallet, pistol. And my fourth Pacífico of the morning.

TWELVE

Feet shuffling above me.

Greetings exchanged.

"We appreciate this."

"What you guys are going through, it's the least I can do."

"We can't be out too long, though."

"Of course. I'll have you guys back in no time. Just a quick escape, recharge the batteries."

The eavesdropping stopped once the boat's engine started. I was surprised at how calm I was. The course was set, the decision made. There was no going back. All I could hope for now was to not fuck things up *too* much.

A half-hour passed before a small door finally opened. Sunlight streamed into the galley. Walt came down the stairs, then quickly shut the door behind him. His eyes were wide—unnaturally, disturbingly wide—which made me wonder how many lines he'd done since we took off. I decided not to ask.

"There's just two of 'em," he said. "The dad and the son."

"Maybe Brody stayed behind to keep watch?"

Walt shrugged. "Maybe."

"I guess that's a good thing, because that means they're still alive, anyway."

"Who's still alive?"

"The women."

"What women?"

"Jesus, Walt. The women from Guatemala: Marysol and the two girls. The whole reason we're doing this."

"Oh, yeah. Yeah, of course," he said, an unsettling smile coming over his face. "You ready?"

I looked at him for a moment. "Are you?"

"Fuckin' A," he said, slapping me on the shoulder. "Giddy up."

While Walt's biochemical state probably should have made me reconsider, the truth is that it didn't. Not at all. I took a deep breath, pulled the gun from my waistband, and stepped up onto the deck. Kevin and Chad were facing away from me, staring out over the water. I took a quick look behind me and saw nothing, not even the distant silhouette of another fishing boat. The Pacific Ocean surrounded us in all directions.

"Hey motherfuckers," I said, and yes, it felt ridiculous even then.

They turned around, and for a brief moment their reactions were normal, casual, whatever. They'd heard some dude's voice, simple as that. Probably just assumed it was Walt.

But then they saw me.

And also the gun in my hand.

Kevin started saying something I couldn't quite make out, mostly because of his son's sudden, high-pitched screaming. Once Chad managed to calm down some, Kevin held out his hands and said, "You don't want to do this. We can work something out."

"We can, yeah. Just tell me what you did with them."

"Did with who?"

I laughed. "Don't do this, dude. Do *not* fucking do this."

"Just tell him, Dad," pleaded Chad. "He's going to fucking kill us!"

"No, he won't, because then he'd never find them. They'd starve to death, all because of Tony."

"Dad, please, just—"

"These guys aren't that smart," said Kevin, a point I couldn't argue. "They're just two losers who couldn't get laid at home, so they move down here and act like they're actually worth a shit."

This comment made me take a quick glance over at Walt, who was standing just a few feet to my right. He'd always been sensitive when it came to jokes about his looks, getting laid, all that kind of shit (of which there were lots to be made). So it wasn't a surprise to see how livid he now was. Probably also didn't help that his wife had left him a few weeks ago.

Kevin, unfortunately, didn't pick up on any of this. He even directed his next line at Walt: "You think you won't be implicated if something happens to us? You think we didn't tell people we were going fishing with you?"

Walt snorted. "You think I give a fuck?"

"You should."

"Look around. I don't see anybody."

"Hey," Chad said, looking at Walt now. "You're the guy from that night... yeah, I saw you..."

Walt looked at him. "What the hell are you talking about?"

"The night, yeah— at the bar. Before we left, the same night—"

"Shut the fuck up!" Walt screamed, suddenly enraged. "Shut *the fuck* up!"

"Just tell us where they are," I said, in the calmest voice I could manage. "We go back to shore, you take us to them. Okay?"

"We can do that," said Kevin. "No problem."

"But first you have to tell us."

"Tell you what?"

"Where they're at. And prove that they're alive. I want pictures. I want an address."

He laughed. The motherfucker *laughed.* How this guy could be completely unaffected by the gun in my hand, I had no idea. (Although: he *was* a rich white dude, so maybe it's just that things had always worked out for him? Or maybe he could tell that the gun wasn't loaded?)

"Don't make this difficult. Just tell us where they are."

"I'll tell you when we're on dry land. You do anything to us, you're killing those girls too."

Things weren't going quite as I'd hoped. While going back to shore and having them take us to the girls wasn't a terrible option, what if they set us up and took us to some undercover cop instead? Before I could think any more about what to do next, I saw that Walt had reappeared with a Louisville Slugger in his hands. Aluminum. Thirty-four inches, thirty-one ounces. Based on his build, my guess was that he probably hit fifth in the lineup growing up. Not good enough for clean-up, but he could connect and do some damage from time to time.

And in this particular scenario, Chad's right knee was a fastball down the middle of the plate. Walt didn't miss. The kid immediately fell to the deck, clutching at his leg, screaming.

The arrogance Kevin had managed up to this point was gone in an instant. Now it was just pure fucking terror. He looked down at his son, then back up at Walt. "Listen listen *listen*—"

But Walt wasn't interested in listening. He was ready for his second at-bat. He swung again, this time connecting with Kevin's left knee. Contact wasn't quite as solid as his first swing, but it did some damage. Kevin let out a scream but managed to stay upright, which ended up working against him. Walt loaded up and took another swing, aiming higher now. Based on the sound at impact—and also the one Kevin let out afterwards—I could only assume that his elbow had shattered into a thousand pieces. He collapsed onto the deck, right next to his son.

Walt wasn't finished. He switched sports then, started playing a little *fútbol*. He didn't have on steel-toed boots or anything, but a kick to the face with a New Balance cross trainer is still a kick to the face. Though their shattered joints made it difficult, both McBrides eventually curled themselves into versions of the fetal position.

I just stood there while all of this was happening, frozen in place, shocked by what I was witnessing. I'd never seen this side of Walt before. I'd never seen this side of *anyone* before.

The kicking didn't stop until Walt stubbed his toe.

"Please…" Kevin murmured. The man was barely recognizable, lying there next to his unconscious son. "I'll tell…" Using his one good arm, he reached into his pocket and pulled out his phone. Despite the beating he just received, the phone was still functional. I walked over and bent down next to him.

"You're keeping them in an Airbnb?" I said, after he opened the app.

"Entire house…" he said, his voice barely above a whisper. "One month…"

Behind me I could hear Chad starting to stir, regaining consciousness. Walt apparently noticed this too, because a second later he turned around and kicked the kid square in the face. Kevin was so far out of it he didn't react. I glanced up at Walt and mouthed *What the fuck*. His response: a big, toothy smile.

I turned back to Kevin. "Is Brody at the house with them?"

He nodded.

"Anyone else?"

"No, I think… my arm…"

Before he could say anything else, the Louisville Slugger slammed into his other arm.

"Jesus Christ, Walt!"

He laughed, turned around, and went below deck. A moment later he came back up with a spool of fishing line.

"What are you doing?" I asked, stomach sinking.

"What needs to be done," he said, and then he began wrapping the fishing line around Chad. First his ankles and legs, then his torso and arms.

"No no no no… Walt, no— Jesus Christ— no, dude— we can't do this…"

He paid no attention to my protests.

And I made no move to stop him.

Once he was done with Chad, he stood up and kicked Kevin in the head a couple of times, until the older McBride was also unconscious. Then came the same fishing line treatment.

After that he brought up two sets of chains.

Then two anvils.

Too much. Way too fucking much. I walked over and grabbed his arm. He turned around and looked at me as if nothing at all was out of the ordinary. It was bizarre. It was terrifying.

"We can't do this," I said. "We *cannot* do this."

"What other option do we have? You really think we can go back in with them looking like this? We're completely fucked if we do that."

"We could take them to the Airbnb, let them recover there."

He laughed. "We nurse them back to health and then they'll just forget about this? They'll just move on with their lives?"

He was right, which made me wonder if I'd known this all along, that this was the inevitable end to the outing—the fishing line, the anvils—and that maybe deep down I was okay with that.

I didn't move as I watched Walt drag the bodies to the back of the boat. The deck was slick, which made the whole process seem way too easy. He lifted Kevin up, leaned him against the side of the boat, and then picked up the anvil. I didn't move at all, not an inch, not even when Walt dropped the anvil into the water. A second later Kevin was overboard, out of sight. Bubbles came to the surface. Eventually they disappeared.

Next it was Chad's turn. While Kevin had remained unconscious throughout, Chad was awake now, groaning, muttering, "What's happening?"

"You're going for a little swim, buddy," Walt said, before dropping the anvil into the water.

"What?" said Chad, just before getting pulled over the side of the boat.

More bubbles. Then none.

Walt didn't say a word as he walked past me. He just started the engine, and off we went. A minute later he yelled back and asked if I wanted a beer. I shook my head. He reached into a cooler and pulled out a Corona for himself.

Back at the jetties, he grabbed a hose and started spraying down the boat. Casual as could be, ho hum, on his fourth beer at this point. "Give me a few minutes and I'll be ready," he said.

"For what?"

He smiled. "The Airbnb."

"Maybe it's best if I take care of that one myself. You've done enough."

He stopped spraying and looked over at me. There was still some blood on the deck. "You sure?"

THIRTEEN

Four people now, dead because of me.

Because of things I'd done.

Decisions I'd made.

Four fucking people.

Three of them might have been terrible human beings, but who was I to play judge, jury, and executioner? It was my gun that had gone off in the woods, and then it was me who looked on as two people got wrapped in fishing line and dumped into the Pacific Ocean. My actions—and my inaction—would haunt me forever.

But I couldn't start torturing myself. Not yet.

My new phone sat upright in the cup holder, guiding me to a destination thirty miles north of Punta Cita, to a rural town called San Carlos, which I didn't know existed up until an hour ago. The final turn-off to the Airbnb looked more like a hiking trail than a road meant for any sort of vehicle. But off I went, tree branches scratching the sides of my truck as I bounced from pothole to pothole. After a few minutes of this, it dawned on me that I'd get there faster if I just walked the rest of the way. It'd probably also be a good idea if Brody didn't hear me coming.

Twenty minutes later a small clearing came into sight, then a cabin. I crouched behind a tree and pulled the pistol from my waistband. It wasn't until the gun was in my hand—a bit heavier than before—that I realized I hadn't planned much beyond this point (the problem with trying to block out anxious thoughts is that you also miss out on some useful ones). All I could do now was improvise. Given my recent track record, this wasn't exactly ideal.

Careful to stay hidden behind the tree line, I started creeping around the edge of the clearing. Was there a way for me to approach the place without getting spotted? The cabin itself was your standard setup: one floor, windows on each side, front porch, back patio. While this recon lap allowed me to get a nice look at everything, it didn't provide me with any meaningful insights. Waiting until it got dark would be one option, but if I did that, Brody would know something was up. I also didn't know what condition the women were in, and whether an additional few hours would make a difference.

Just as I was contemplating a fuck-it sort of approach—sprinting towards the cabin and kicking the door down—Square Face stepped out onto the front porch. He reached into his pocket, pulled out a pack of cigarettes. After he lit one, he started walking towards one end of the porch—towards me. If he would have looked up and examined the tree line, he might have seen me. But he didn't. He got to the rail and leaned forward, staring down at the ground as he smoked. A minute later he straightened up, turned around, and slowly started walking towards the other end of the porch.

I moved without thinking, taking off towards the cabin. Right away it felt like my hamstrings were about to pop (and also my knees, and ankles, and several other body parts). I was half-lunging, half-running, trying to make each step land as quietly as possible. And it actually seemed to be working—Brody still hadn't turned around.

But then halfway there (fifty feet down, fifty to go), the phone in my pocket started buzzing. Kevin's phone. A half-second later it started ringing.

Brody turned around with a start, eyes wide. My only option was to keep moving: less lunging now, more running. He sprinted towards the front door, getting there just a few steps ahead of me. He got inside and even managed to shut the door behind him. I reached for the handle and pulled, but it was already locked.

I pulled out Kevin's phone and watched as notifications streamed in: calls, texts, e-mails, news. I'd apparently gotten within range of the cabin's Wi-Fi, which had caused the phone to automatically connect. I felt a strong urge to spike the goddamn thing against the porch, but instead of doing that, I tossed it through the window beside the front door. Then I used the broom on the porch to knock away the remaining glass. Before I could think any better of this approach, I was climbing through the window frame.

"Where are they, Brody?" I yelled once I got inside, somewhat surprised that I hadn't already been tackled, or shot.

No response.

Silence. No more notifications, either. (Or maybe the phone was just broken?)

I looked around at the open living area: TV, couch, dining table, small kitchen. Simple furniture, few decorations, no people. I walked towards a small hallway to my left. There were three doors leading off from it, two of which were shut. The open one was a bathroom, which appeared empty.

"The cops are on their way," I yelled out, inching my way further down the hallway, gun out in front of me like I was an extra on *Law & Order*. "It's over, Brody. You hear me?"

A few seconds later one of the two closed doors started to open, and there stood Paloma, duct tape all over her body. Mouth, arms, legs. For a brief moment I wondered how she was managing to stay upright, but then I noticed that Brody was standing right behind her. A second later he raised a gun to her head.

"Back the *fuck* up," he said.

"You do anything to her, I pull the trigger. And you better hope you die, because if not, motherfucker, I'm gonna have some fun with you," I said, though I had no idea where these words had come from, or whether I was being serious. Was this all an act? Or was this who I was now?

The look in Paloma's eyes made one thing clear: she was on the verge of a panic attack. Wrapped in duct tape, gun against her head, leaning against the man who raped her. She also might have had some (reasonable) concerns about my aim.

"Where are they?" he asked, covered in sweat, breathing heavily.

"Who?"

"Kevin and Chad."

"Leading the police here right now. So if I was you, I wouldn't add another murder to your rap sheet."

"I didn't kill that surf instructor—"

"Javy," I said. "His name was Javy."

"I didn't kill him, I swear."

"Okay, sure. We can talk about it. Let's talk about it. But first you gotta put the gun down, let her go."

"You first."

"Fuck you," I said.

"How do I know you won't just shoot me?"

"How do I know *you* won't shoot *me*?"

"You killed Travis."

"I did," I said, after a brief pause. "You're right."

"You should have to pay for that."

"I agree."

"Then—"

Suddenly there was a loud wheezing sound. Paloma. The stress of the situation combined with the duct tape wrapped around her mouth meant that not enough oxygen was getting into her system. She was hyperventilating.

"She's about to pass out," I said. "Get the tape off her mouth!"

"What the— what are you doing?" Brody said to her, as if she might be able to answer. She was losing strength in her legs, and he was struggling to keep her upright.

"Take the fucking tape off!" I yelled, inching towards them, just ten feet between us now.

Paloma's eyes closed halfway, then rolled back into her head.

She'd passed out, but Brody wasn't ready for the sudden change in the balance and distribution of her weight. He tried keeping her upright, but gravity and physics took over. Without all the duct tape, she probably would have just crumpled to the ground. But the tape made her too stiff; her body simply couldn't bend. She slipped through his grasp, twisting slightly before falling forward and landing on her shoulder.

After watching her fall, Brody looked up at me. His gun was at his side, pointed down towards the floor. But I had remained in character: two hands on my gun, arms out in front of me.

"Don't," I said.

He stood there, eyes wide, staring at me.

"Don't," I repeated. "Please. Just put it down. It's over."

Maybe these words weren't the right ones to say, or maybe nothing I could have said would have made a difference.

He lifted his gun.

I pulled the trigger.

☼

Muffled screaming from down the hall. I stepped around Paloma, jumped over Brody. Inside a bedroom were Marysol and Luisa, lying on twin beds, their bodies also covered with duct tape.

"Está bien, está bien," I said, rushing over and removing the tape from Marysol's mouth. "It's okay, it's okay."

"¿Paloma está bien?" she asked, sheer terror on her face. *"¿Está bien?"*

"Sí sí, tranquila. Está bien."

After helping her get free from all the tape, she jumped up and ran out into the hallway. Her scream echoed for what seemed like a full minute.

I turned to Luisa next. After getting the tape off her mouth, I asked if she was okay. She nodded but didn't say anything. Once she was free from the tape, I followed her out into the hallway. She had no discernible reaction to Brody's body lying there, stepping around him as if he was just a pile of dirty clothes.

Marysol was sitting on the ground, her daughter's head cradled in her lap. Fortunately, Paloma was awake now, eyes open. Marysol stroked her hair, crying softly as she sang a lullaby. Luisa kneeled down next to them, then started removing the tape from Paloma's legs.

I shuffled past them and sat down at the kitchen table, positioning myself so that I was facing away from them. I put my gun on the table and just kind of stared at it for a while—one minute, five minutes, I don't know. Eventually I felt a hand on my shoulder, which startled me so much I nearly reached for the pistol.

I looked up to find Marysol standing beside me.

"*¿Qué puedo hacer?*"

"What do you mean?"

"To help," she said, gesturing towards the hallway, "with him."

"I think maybe we should just go to the police, and—"

"*¿Por qué?*"

"I can't ask you to cover this up," I said, standing up now. "To lie and—"

"You saved our lives."

I shook my head. "I'm the reason all this happened in the first place."

"*Tony, venga, venga...*" she said, wrapping her arms around me.

I closed my eyes and hugged her back.

"What happened to the other two?" she asked, taking a step back.

"They're..." I started. "You don't have to worry about them anymore."

Her face didn't change. She just nodded and said, "What do we do now?"

I almost laughed. *"No tengo ni puta idea."*

But Marysol wasn't quite so helpless. She had a plan, and we got to work. Using a bed sheet, trash bags, and some leftover duct tape, we wrapped Brody's body and carried it into the woods behind the cabin. I spent the next few hours digging a hole while the women went back inside to clean up. It wasn't six feet down, not even close, but it would have to suffice. There was a soft, muted thud when I rolled the body down into the hole. Without looking down into the makeshift grave, I started filling it back in. After scattering some rocks and leaves over the area—so that everything would look at least somewhat natural, I hoped—exhaustion took hold and I fell to my knees. I probably would have cried if I had the energy, but instead I just stayed there on my knees, staring down at what I'd done.

Eventually I stood up and made my way back to the cabin. Given how dark it had gotten, this proved to be fairly difficult. But I managed. The women were just finishing cleaning up—but not just where the body had been. They'd sterilized the entire place.

With the help of a flashlight we found in a closet, we made our way out to my truck, about a half-mile away. No one said anything during the walk, and the ride to Punta Cita was just as quiet. The three of them all somehow managed to fit in the front seat beside me.

I pulled over about a half-mile before we reached town, which had become standard procedure for me at this point. The three women slid out the passenger side, then shut the door behind them. Before I could drive away, Marysol walked around the front of the truck, over to my window.

"We escaped," she said. "That's what we'll say. We don't know where we were, and we also don't know what happened to the men. They probably ran off when they figured out we'd escaped."

It was believable enough. "Okay."

"Tony," she said, squeezing my arm with both of her hands. "*Gracias.*"

After hiding my gun out by my favorite tree, I went to my house (no sentries were standing guard, thank god), where I immediately walked out back and took my clothes off. I put everything into the chimenea, poured some lighter fluid, and lit a match. Fire still burning, I went inside and took an hour-long shower. I dried off and put on a pair of shorts, then grabbed a beer and walked back out to the chimenea. I poured some more lighter fluid, struck another match. Then I sat down in my white plastic chair and rolled a joint. Smoked it as the flames burned.

FOURTEEN

Once the sexual assaults and subsequent kidnappings came to light, decision-makers at Rox News seemed to lose interest in their "Justice for Travis" features. Carrie Owens and her crew packed up and flew back to New York just a few hours after Marysol reported what happened to police (a version of it, anyway). In an ideal world, Carrie would have stuck around and covered the women's stories, but that would have required the network admitting that it had *seriously* fucked up by believing the McBride family's version of events. And since the women from Guatemala didn't speak English, Carrie would have had difficulty exploiting their trauma during interview segments. And if you can't do that, what's the point?

Since Kevin, Brody, and Chad all disappeared at the same time Marysol reported the crimes to police, people started wondering if Travis had *actually* been murdered. Maybe he was just in hiding somewhere? Had this been some sort of scam to garner media attention? Helping this rumor spread more than anything else was the fact that there was still no body, and Mateo had only ever admitted to watching the three bros get marched off into the woods. He stayed quiet for over a week, which ended up being his saving grace—and mine, too. He got released the same day the kidnapping was reported by Marysol.

While most Mexican officials seemed vindicated by the developments—*The gringos are the liars, not us!*—Juan Martín Rodriguez was not among this group. He knew he wasn't getting the full story. This agitated him a great deal. He was the kind of guy used to getting complete answers, not just partial ones. He still wanted to know what happened with Travis McBride. He also wanted to know about the flat tire (Mateo's story made little sense), where the Americans had gone (with no trace whatsoever?), and how exactly the girls managed to escape (their story lacked details). Paloma and Luisa didn't offer much, taking on their rightful roles as victims who didn't feel like reliving their traumatic experiences. Marysol didn't offer much either, and the details she did provide—both the real ones and the ones she made up—didn't change between retellings. She didn't have any idea where the gringos had run off to, and no customs agency had reported any of the three Americans coming or going (or would it have been *four* Americans?). But Mexico's a huge country, and there were plenty of places they could have been hiding out within its borders. I figured the narrative might change once investigators discovered the Airbnb—which, of course, they eventually did. They found traces of blood but didn't have enough to go on. Or they didn't want to go on it. Something like that. And Walt was a dead end: he said he'd never even met the guys, let alone taken them out on his boat.

Gilberto stopped by my place after the search of the Airbnb had been conducted. He even knocked this time.

"So they don't have anything to go on?" I asked, relieved, but also confused as to why he'd come by my house to tell me all of this.

"They'll test the blood they found, but according to what Marysol said, we already know who it will belong to."

"Yeah?"

Marysol told officials that the guys had gotten into a heated argument about something, and that this had led to a physical altercation of some sort. It was during this time that the women managed to work themselves free and run away.

"I was wondering how they managed to escape," I said.

"I'm sure."

We were sitting on my couch, ceiling fan spinning above us, each of us nursing a Pacífico. "So what happens now?"

He shrugged. "Besides having an alert out with customs officials, there's not much we can do."

"Seriously? That's it?"

"You got any suggestions?"

I didn't have an answer for this question, the same way I didn't have an answer for how they still hadn't found Travis's body. There'd been countless search parties. It made no sense. Even if an animal had gotten to it first, there'd be remains *somewhere*.

"What about Detective Rodriguez?" I asked. "You think he's, I don't know... content?"

"Juan Martín? Hell no. I mean, he'll go back to Mexico City for now, but if something new develops or the guys show up somewhere, he'll be back." He sounded miserable when saying this, which served as a nice reminder: he feared the federales nearly as much as I did.

I held up my beer. "Well, here's to hoping he never steps foot in Punta Cita again."

"Saludos."

"Saludos."

A relatively comfortable silence ensued, though plenty remained unsaid between the two of us. I hadn't told him about my boat trip, nor my visit out to the Airbnb. But he probably knew most of it (or at least strongly suspected most of it), and my initial assumption was that he'd come over to get more money out of me. But now I wasn't so sure. He finished off his beer and started tracing the top of the can with his finger. "Something still doesn't make sense. The story about Javy, how he died. It just..."

"Yeah, no shit. He was killed," I said, a bit too self-righteously, given recent events. "Whether it was Brody or all three of them, I don't know, but they're responsible, I know it."

He shook his head. "That's where I think you're wrong."

"There's no way Javy fell and—"

"I got a call the other day," he said. "From Russia."

"Russia?"

"A person who used to live around here, up until a few weeks ago."

"What?"

"You know her."

It took a few seconds, but finally it dawned on me: "Walt's ex-wife? Natalya?"

"She heard about what happened to Javy."

"Okay?"

"Apparently Walt hasn't been entirely forthright about why she left Mexico."

It was like he needed me to say something between each piece of the puzzle he offered up, otherwise he wouldn't be able to continue. "How so?"

"She told me she'd been seeing Javy."

"Jesus Christ. For how long?"

"I don't know, but eventually Walt found out."

"When?"

"I'm not sure of the exact date, but he threatened her, threatened Javy. Said he was going to kill them, kill himself. Just fucking lost it, basically. So she snuck away when he was out on a charter, flew back to Russia."

"Because she was afraid of what he might do?"

"Pretty much. But her plan was to eventually make her way back to Mexico, to be with Javy somewhere. Just not in Punta Cita."

"Because of Walt."

He nodded. "Because of Walt."

Even though the answer was staring me in the face, I asked the question, "What are you implying?"

"I really need to spell it out for you?"

"My brain's been operating a bit slow as of late," I said, which was quite an understatement. "So maybe you better."

"I think Javy was killed, but I don't think the crew from California had anything to do with it. I think Walt killed him."

I thought back to that last night at La Hija's with Javy. He'd mentioned a woman but hadn't told me her name. "How sure are you about this?"

"I can't say I'm a hundred percent, but it makes sense. The pieces are all right there."

Out on Walt's boat, it all seemed so natural to him. Wrapping a couple guys in fishing line, dumping their bodies into the ocean. Casual as could be, like it was just some catch-and-release charter.

"I could tell something was off when I was interviewing them," Gilberto continued.

"Who?"

"The guys from California. When we brought up the rumors about the sexual assaults, I knew they were guilty. It was plain as day. But then whenever Javy's death was mentioned, it was different."

"How so?"

He shrugged. "Their faces. I could tell they were telling the truth."

After a brief moment, I asked, "Why are you telling me all this?"

Gilberto leaned forward and put his empty can on the coffee table. "I could ask Walt to come in and answer a few questions, but that's about all I could do. It's just a theory of mine at this point. I don't have any evidence, and I probably never will. Plus, as soon as I start poking around and asking questions—where he was that night, motives, shit like that—he'll be out of here. He's smarter than you like that."

"But that doesn't really answer my question."

"Sure it does."

"Are you suggesting I—"

"I'm not suggesting anything. And Tony," he said, struggling now to get up from the couch. "I was never here, *¿me entiendes?*"

☼

I parked along the side of the road, pulled out a small flashlight, and made my way through the woods. I found the tree, kneeled down, and started digging. A minute later I was tucking the Colt into my waistband.

I tried his house first. No one there.

Next came Carlita's, then Vicente's. Both were pleased to tell me they hadn't seen him. Even folks at Barco Blanco seemed happy to report that he hadn't been around. I started worrying he might have caught wind of something and skipped town, even though it wasn't like Gilberto was going around and sharing his suspicions with anyone else.

I walked down to the jetties next. The *Natalya* was there but Walt wasn't. Back in town, I saw Rick Barnes walking along Calle Dorado. Rick was Walt's best (and perhaps only) friend in Punta Cita. They'd grown up together, in some suburb outside of Calgary. Rick had moved to Punta Cita about a year ago, right after his divorce was finalized (his wife had left him for one of his best friends; in fact, the guy had been in their wedding). Rick was still grieving the relationship when he moved down here, and upon his arrival he discovered two things in short order: the power of crack cocaine, and the power of the Canadian dollar in Mexico, particularly when it comes to purchasing large quantities of crack cocaine. I hadn't seen Rick in weeks, maybe even months. There was a chance he'd been squirreled away in his house on a weeks-long bender: blinds closed, paranoid, shut off from the world. In fact, this was the most likely scenario. But there was still an off chance he might know something about Walt.

"How you been, Rick?"

The simple question seemed to startle him. He stopped walking and looked up at me. It took a moment for everything to register: who I was, where he was, the meaning of the words he'd just heard.

"Tony, my man. *¿Qué pasa, hermano?* You wanna grab a *cerveza*?"

Rick's Spanish was offensive, even to me. He was an over-the-top caricature of the stereotypical gringo.

"Maybe tomorrow," I said. "But hey, do you happen to know where Walt is?"

"Barco Blanco probably."

"I was just there."

"His place? Down on his boat?"

"I checked both."

He shrugged. "Got me, man."

"No idea? None at all?"

"I mean, I saw him earlier. But that was, like… you know, earlier."

"Where?"

"I don't know, he was in his truck."

"Do you know where he was going?"

"Shit, that's right," he said, snapping his fingers. "Fuck! I should've gone with him."

"Gone where?"

"Puerto."

"Where at in Puerto?"

"That one place he loves, I forget the name. You know it?"

I did. "You sure?"

"Pretty sure. Why? You wanna go? I'll drive."

"Next time," I said, grabbing his shoulder, finding nothing but bone. "Thanks, Ricky."

☼

Two hours to Puerto.

Walt's favorite establishment: Para Los Caballeros. Translation: *For the Gentlemen*.

Terrible name. Terrible place.

I parked my truck, walked in, and ordered a beer at the bar. It was mostly dark inside, with the only real light coming from up on stage. It took a while, but eventually I managed to make out Walt's silhouette. Front row, dead center. I should have expected as much.

Not much happened over the next couple of hours: I sat at the bar, nursing beers, looking on as Walt downed about a dozen gin and tonics. I was about to ask the bartender for something stronger myself when Walt stood up and made his way over to the side of the stage. After handing a security guard a few bills, he headed through a door leading towards the back.

I paid off my tab and headed out the front exit, then walked across the street and stood underneath a small cluster of trees. Ten minutes later Walt stepped through a side exit, holding hands with a woman who had just recently been up on stage. They walked towards the motel next door, El Pelicano. Room #107, ground floor. Walt smacked the woman's ass, then followed her into the room. I could see their shadows through the drapes for a brief moment, but then they quickly fell out of view.

Now I just had to wait for the woman to leave. Then I'd go into the room, do what I came to do. It seemed fairly straightforward—nothing too complicated, not a bad plan—until the woman's shadow reappeared in the window. Then came Walt's shadow. I couldn't tell if they were dancing or doing some weird sexual shit. Whatever the case, I didn't want to subject myself to the visual. But just before I could turn away, I caught a glimpse of something flashing across the window: Walt's arm. Then it was his other arm, from the other direction. Slapping, punching, something. My first thought: *Is this some sort of BDSM?* Second thought: *Shit.*

I took off towards the room, feet on autopilot. The door was locked, but it was a cheap lock and a thin door, so all it took was a few hard shoulders to get the thing open.

Inside was your standard motel room: bed, nightstand, TV, bathroom. The woman was wearing a white thong. Nothing else. Nose bloody, cheeks red. Fucking terrified. Walt stood beside her in his tighty whities, pistol in his right hand.

"Tony!" he yelled, raising the gun and gesturing for me to shut the broken but still functional door behind me. "*Great* to fucking see you!"

He shoved the woman onto the bed and walked over to the nightstand. He dipped his finger into what looked like a few hundred dollars' worth of blow. One nostril, then the other. Somehow he managed to keep his pistol aimed in my general direction throughout all of this, which led me to the belated realization that

I probably should have pulled out my own before charging inside.

"It's funny, man. I've been trying to get you to come out here for years," he said, pulling back the drapes, peeking outside. "But now here you are, out of the blue."

"Here I am."

"And I think I know why."

"Oh, yeah?"

He smiled. "You come with anybody?"

"Just me."

He cocked the pistol, pointed it at me. Aiming for my nose, if I had to guess. "That fat ass Gilberto isn't out there?"

"No one is, I swear," I said, though I immediately regretted these words. I probably should have lied and at least pretended like I had some backup.

The pistol pointed at me was plenty terrifying in its own right, but the most troubling thing was the look in Walt's eyes. The man was on a different planet.

"There are some things you just don't do, Tony," he said, though he did at least—thank god—lower the pistol. "And one of them is sleep with another man's wife. You feel me?"

I nodded. "You're right, absolutely."

"How could you be friends with someone like that?" He stopped pacing and stared at me with this helpless look on his face, like he was genuinely at a loss for words.

"You're right—it's shitty. But that doesn't mean Javy deserved to die."

"Yeah, well," he said, walking over to the terrified woman curled up on the bed. "Sometimes life isn't fair." He raised the pistol and whipped it across her face.

"Jesus fucking Christ, Walt!" I said, taking a few steps towards him.

He spun around and pointed the gun at me. "Stop *fucking* moving."

I froze, then watched as he walked back over to the nightstand. Dipped a finger, refueled. This wasn't going to end well, not if we kept heading down this path. Just standing here and chatting with him wasn't going to resolve anything.

"Dude," I said, going with the first thing that came to mind. "What's up with your nose?"

"What?"

"It's bleeding."

Walt reached for his nose, then checked his hand for blood. There wasn't any. "What?"

"You're fucking bleeding, man," I said, with some more urgency this time. "Jesus Christ..."

He checked again. Still nothing. "What the fuck?"

A sink and small mirror were just outside the bathroom. Walt rushed over and tilted his head back, examining his nose. "I don't see any blood. What the fuck are you—"

I pulled the trigger just as he was turning around. He fell backwards into the bathroom, though he somehow managed to fire off three rounds in the process (two ended up in the room next door, one in the room above). Gun out in front of me, I inched my way towards him. His legs were sticking out from the bathroom, but that was all I could see of him.

"Walt, it's over," I said, continuing towards him.

"Fuck you," he said, voice different now, his coke-fueled energy gone.

I figured I could probably just leave and let him bleed out, but that might give police enough time to get here. Even if he didn't survive, he might use his final breaths to tell an EMT who'd shot him. I continued towards the bathroom, until I could peek around the corner.

Bloody mess. Everything below his chest was covered in red. Head tilted to the side, eyes barely open. Gun still in his hand.

My stomach dropped, and then it dropped some more when I heard the faint sound of police sirens. I needed to hurry up.

I reached around the corner and aimed the Colt at Walt's head. He either heard or saw me do this—his head didn't move, but his eyes did. A small grin was forming on his face when I pulled the trigger for a second time.

When I turned around, I was surprised to find the woman still in the room, standing with her back against the farthest wall. Fucked up on coke, scared to death. Probably in shock.

"*Sal de aquí,*" I said. "*Ahora.*"

I ran outside, half expecting the parking lot to already be full of cop cars. None were there, but the sirens kept getting louder. I ran to my truck and pulled it into the alley behind the motel. I drove—fast but not too fast. The sirens slowly faded, until I couldn't hear them at all. I kept glancing in my rearview, all but certain I'd find a police car speeding up behind me, red and blue lights flashing. But none ever did.

I considered dumping the gun somewhere. God knows I should have. I could have thrown it into the ocean. Or a river, a dumpster. I could have picked some random spot in the jungle, dug a hole, and never gone back there again. But I didn't. I kept it right there on the seat next to me, until I pulled over at the spot I'd been to several times before. Flashlight in hand, I made my way through the woods. The tree was easy to find now. Three rocks, right there. I wiped the gun down, put it in a plastic bag, and buried it. Then I smoothed over the dirt, rearranged the rocks.

Back at my place, I took a thirty-minute shower. Then I grabbed a beer and sat outside, where I smoked a joint and watched another fire burn in my chimenea. I'd have to go shopping soon, get some new clothes.

FIFTEEN

Walt's death was chalked up to a drug deal gone bad. According to local gossip, his charter fishing company was really just a front for his real business: drug trafficking. He'd meet boats far out in the Pacific, then return to shore with coke, heroin, and fentanyl. I was delighted to hear all these rumors, because that meant people were buying the bullshit *I* had started. The chatter eventually grew so loud that a special drug unit came to town to search the *Natalya*. They said it was cleanest boat they'd ever seen—so clean, in fact, that the only explanation for why it would be so clean was that Walt had something to hide. When an expat from New Jersey explained all of this to me over a couple beers at Barco Blanco, I nodded along, saying everything made perfect sense. I told him I couldn't think of any other reason—none at all—as to why Walt's boat would have been so clean. He'd been running contraband. Simple as that. But then he pissed off the wrong person, got himself killed.

The owner of Para Los Caballeros posted a message on the club's Facebook page denying all speculation that one of the club's dancers had gone back to the motel with Walt. "We're not that kind of place," he wrote. (The most-liked comment: *Yeah, because they usually just fuck backstage?*) The woman Walt had allegedly been hanging around with that night—well, it's funny, because no one at the club could seem to recall her name. And come to think of it, they couldn't be sure if Walt had even been backstage. Hell, was he even *at* the club that night?

The cops knew they were getting lied to by everyone, but I don't think they really gave a shit. There were three shells missing from the gun in Walt's hand and a pile of blow on the nightstand. Two plus fucking two. Walt was no angel, and his toxicology report indicated that he had more cocaine flowing through his blood stream than actual blood. Investigators chatted with a few local dealers, all of whom claimed they'd never met the guy. I imagined these interactions all looking fairly similar.

EXT. STREET CORNER - NIGHT

A COP walks up to a DEALER, holds out a photo. Both men seem disinterested. They'd rather be anywhere but here, doing anything but this.

COP: You ever sell to this guy?

The dealer shakes his head. Doesn't even glance at the photo.

DEALER: Nope.

COP: Great. Thanks for your time.

The cop pockets the picture, walks away.

END SCENE

The only person who seemed genuinely upset about Walt's death was Rick Barnes. But it wasn't so much that his friend was dead—it was that Walt had been holding out on him.

"You really think he was running all that stuff?" he asked me. "For the Colombians?"

"You know," I said. "It does make sense."

"How long you think he'd been doing it?"

I shrugged. "Probably years."

Looked like the poor dude might cry.

☼

But not everyone bought into the rumors. I hadn't heard from Kerstin in a couple of weeks, ever since I asked her to convince the McBrides to go fishing with Walt. She'd ignored all of my communication attempts (five texts, three phone calls, two voicemails), and it was like that—radio silence—until

I received a text from her, asking me if I'd like to grab dinner. I said sure, that'd be great, looking forward to it.

She was already at the table when I walked in, her gaze fixed out over the water.

"Hey," I said, startling her. She smiled and stood up, but the hug was awkward and the kiss even worse (I went for lips, she went for cheek). Small talk was made easier by a bottle of wine, but the conversation was stilted and unnatural.

"It's been a weird few weeks," I said.

"Bit of an understatement there."

In the uncomfortable silence that followed—this one seemed particularly bad, even worse than all those that had preceded it—our meals finally arrived (grilled shrimp salad for her, ceviche for me). I unrolled my silverware and put the napkin on my lap, the first time I'd done so in years. That's how bad things were.

"Wow, this looks great," I said, hoping this simple banality might ease the tension, help us move on to talking about the weather or some shit. But when I looked across the table, I saw that she hadn't moved. Head down, staring at her salad.

"You okay?"

"I have to leave," she said.

"Oh, shit. Feeling sick?"

"No, I mean… I need to leave, like, Punta Cita. I just… I can't deal with all this, Tony."

"It's over now," I said, after a moment. "All this—all the craziness. I promise."

She lifted her head and looked across the table at me. "They didn't just run off, did they?"

"Kerstin..."

"Actually," she said, somewhere between laughing and crying, "please don't answer that."

"I wish none of this would've happened. Fucking *none* of it."

"But it did. And I'm in the middle of it, having dinner with someone who... did some pretty terrible things."

"You're right," I said. "But that's on me, not you. You didn't do anything wrong."

"What about the fishing trip?"

"That wasn't what you think."

"What was it then?"

My turn to look away.

Kerstin grabbed the bottle of wine, poured herself another glass. "It's the opposite of what I was after when I moved here— stress, anxiety, constant worry— I just— I can't anymore."

"How long will you be gone?"

"I don't know."

"When?"

"Tomorrow."

"Wow, that's— yeah, that's soon. Where you going?"

"Stockholm." She let out a long breath, picked up her fork. "I'll stay with a friend for a while, until I figure out what's next."

"What about your studio?"

"I'm not sure, to be honest."

"I can watch over it, if you want. If you'd be comfortable with that."

She shrugged, non-committal. Both of us started eating then: staring down at our plates, chewing too much, conscious of every swallow. We asked the waiter for another bottle of cab, but beyond that not much was said. It wasn't until I was on my fourth glass that I found the courage to try to lighten things up a bit. "Remember that time we took a boat out to Playa Hermosa? Then ran out of gas on the way back?"

She shook her head, smiling, plenty of booze in her now too. "I honestly thought we were going to die."

"Yeah, I do remember you saying 'We are going to *fucking* die' about a thousand times."

"Yet you stayed so calm."

"I was faking it. I was scared shitless."

"I figured it was an act."

"I was also drunk."

"Also figured that."

Off we went then, and it was thanks to nostalgia's powerful, distorting filter that we looked back on our years of semi-togetherness and saw only good times. We took turns telling fictionalized versions of past events and laughing at the genius of our own inside jokes. We got to feeling so good we even ordered desert, *tres leches* for both of us. Afterwards we stood outside the restaurant. Her place was to the right; mine was to the left. At any point over the past two years, we would have walked in the same direction. Wouldn't have even thought about it. Tonight, of course, was different.

"Take care, Tony," she said, stiff and formal all of a sudden, like she hadn't had a drop of booze. "And please... be careful."

"You too," I said, the first (and only) words that came to mind.

She reached out and touched my shoulder, then turned around and walked away. Just like that. I stood there and watched, waiting for her to turn around and wave, smile... something. She never did.

I walked down Calle Dorado and took a seat at the bar at La Hija's, where I drank enough tequila to ruin the next several days. I woke up the next morning and downed a half-bottle of Tylenol. Then I spent the next few hours drinking Pedialyte and wondering what the hell I was doing with my life. I gave up on all that a little after noon—both the electrolytes and the existential quandaries—and transitioned to the hair of the dog approach, which, based on my personal experience, had a success rate of 100%. Two beers from my fridge to start, then a bit of tequila. Then a lot of tequila.

The next few days I fought through hangovers and forced myself to paddle out each morning, though I didn't catch many waves. Then I hung out in various bars throughout the afternoon, restricting myself to only beer (my version of healthy living). A few expats still seemed to want to dissect everything that happened over the past few weeks, but there was also a growing desire in the community to move on from all the madness and get back to normal.

It was Vicente who pointed out something that hadn't yet crossed my mind: while interest in Walt's murder might have already faded, the disappearance of the four Americans would eventually attract more attention—like, *a lot* of attention. These guys had friends and families, after all, and they'd want to know what the hell had happened.

"Unless they're alive," he said, "and secretly in contact with them."

"Yeah," I said. "Maybe."

I wondered when this other shoe might drop, and what that might mean for me.

And, for once, an answer came easily: nothing good.

☼

About a week after Kerstin left, I ran into Carlos at a corner tienda. He said I should come out to the farm, have dinner one night. I said sure, yeah, that'd be great, and a couple nights later I was walking out to the Reyes farm, bottle of tequila in hand.

Carlos was waiting for me outside. He thanked me for the bottle and set it down on the porch. Then he asked me to go on a little walk with him. Said he wanted to show me something. It was a strange request but I just rolled with it. *Sure, okay, yeah.* Also helped that I'd smoked a small joint on the walk out.

We headed over towards his barn but didn't go inside. We walked around it, then through a couple of small fields—potatoes, peppers, more potatoes—

before arriving at the edge of his property. I thought this might mark the end of our journey, but into the woods we went. I didn't ask any questions, and Carlos didn't seem too interested in offering any additional information.

We hiked for quite a while. Legs cut to hell, shirts in tatters. If for some reason Carlos decided to leave me out here, there was little doubt I'd end up dead. We hadn't followed a trail, and there was no way I'd be able to navigate my way back to his place. Felt like we were in the middle of the goddamn jungle. Not that he had any reason to do this, to leave me out here like that. At least none I could think of. *Jesus Christ, did I say something, or—*

He stopped suddenly, glancing back at me. He then nodded towards the ground in front of us. I trained my eyes on what was there: trees, rocks, dirt, plants, vines. All around us, green and brown. Nothing seemed particularly noteworthy or out of place.

I looked over at Carlos, "What am I looking at?"

He pointed.

My eyes tracked the line from his finger, until finally I saw it: the small cross atop the makeshift grave.

☼

I learned a lot that night.

Most notably: Carlos wasn't the kind of guy to waste any time. After Mateo told him about our misadventure—later that night at Vicente's, despite swearing ourselves to secrecy—Carlos drove out to the spot and retrieved Travis's body. He didn't even tell Mateo that he was going to do it. Just put on a headlamp and went to work. The logistics of everything baffled me. How did he manage to do all that by himself? But the far bigger questions revolved around *why* he'd done it. Why put himself at risk? To protect Mateo? To protect me?

Standing next to the makeshift grave, I asked him, bluntly, *"¿Por qué hiciste todo esto?"*

He shrugged. "It needed done."

Back at the Reyes household, I ate enfrijoladas to the point of discomfort. Towards the end of the meal Carlos raised his beer and looked across the table at me. He was at one end and I was at the other, his wife and four kids between us.

"Saludos," he said.

I raised my beer. *"Saludos."*

☼

The next morning I paddled out into conditions perfect for someone with a moderate hangover: chest-high and mellow. In between sets I saw a pod of dolphins swimming nearby, just twenty yards away. I became so mesmerized that the first wave of the next set nearly broke on my head. I paddled up and over it, just barely making it. I did the same with the second wave, and then on the third I pivoted my board and went for it: biggest wave of the day, a little overhead. I was late getting started but paddled hard, digging into the water, shoulders burning. One last stroke, then—on my feet. I made the drop, then the turn at the bottom, a wall of blue awaiting me.

Afterwards, I felt like I always did after a great wave: *things aren't so bad*. Everything was so beautiful—ocean, sky, beach. How could I be so lucky to live here? I looked around as I paddled, forcing myself to soak in as much as I could. I loved it here. This was my home, and no matter what happened—or what might happen—I'd never be able to leave the place.

For better or for worse, with smart money being on the latter.

Continue reading for a preview from the next Tony Winslow novel

NARCO GRINGO

It was right after a good wave, after a long ride I should've made shorter, because then I wouldn't have had to paddle out through so much goddamn white water afterwards. But I'd never been one to bail early, even if a closeout was coming or the wave had turned into ankle-high mush. I'd just keep going, sometimes all the way into shore. It was a stupid habit. Wasn't like I was getting lost in the moment or achieving that Zen-like state many surfers claim can be found when riding a wave. I used to think this was possible—moment of Zen, complete absence of thought—but lately I'd been growing skeptical. For the past six months, whether I was paddling for a wave or getting pummeled by one, I'd still be thinking about the three people I'd killed. And if I wasn't thinking about *them*, I was thinking about the two *other* people I watched get shoved off the side of a boat, miles out in the Pacific, anvils tied to their ankles. While I did nothing.

It was this thought cycle that forced me to at least *try* to focus more on the present moment: sun shining down, sand beneath my feet. Breathe in, breathe out. While this basic premise is straightforward enough and can be the basis for a healthy approach to life, my combination of anxiety and guilt morphed this into a twisted sort of recklessness. I never said no. To anything. Another drink? Of course. A hit? A line? Absolutely. Whatever you got. Yes, please. Let's fucking go. Take me away.

But back to that wave, to the long ride I should've made shorter: had I kicked out sooner, not only would I have avoided the risk of needing yet another ding repair, but I also probably wouldn't have noticed the guy sitting on the beach. Despite a level of humidity one could describe as oppressive and still be vastly understating it, he was wearing blue jeans and a white dress shirt. I knew this man, and he wasn't here to check out the surf.

I jumped off my board into knee-high water, started walking towards shore. Took off my leash and carried my battered 9'6" longboard across the sand.

"¿Qué tal?"

He stood up as I approached. *"Todo bien, ¿y tú?"*

"Bien, bien," I said, though I could tell right away from this brief but stilted exchange that everything was not okay. "What's up?"

"Do you have a minute?" Mateo looked nervous, like the sweat on his face wasn't entirely due to the humidity.

"Of course," I said, leaning my board against the log he was sitting on.

"Creo que…" he trailed off, words not coming easily. "I might need your help with something."

"Anything," I said, and I meant it. I owed Mateo my life. Not only had he helped me carry out the first of my three homicides—for the record, I didn't *want* to kill the guy; I didn't want to kill anybody—but he also kept his mouth shut during the couple of weeks he spent in jail afterwards. He didn't mention my name—not once—and because of this, I was currently walking around as a free man instead of sharing a 9'x6' prison cell with a guy with face tattoos.

He hesitated, looking out over the ocean.

"Seriously, man. Anything," I said. "Just say the word."

And Mateo, well, he said some words.

After he was through, I stared out at the mushy waves still rolling in, at the two Canadian tourists flailing around on 8' soft tops. I wondered if things would ever be normal again, if *I'd* ever be normal again. I missed the days when my biggest concern was whether I was drinking too much (yes, of course, always), even though deep down I knew those times were never coming back. Too much had happened.

I would have screamed if I had the energy. I would have yelled at him and asked him what the fuck he was thinking. But I knew that sometimes—most times—people don't have a choice in these matters. You don't get asked to do something so much as you get told to.

And the money, *man*...

It'd be easy for me to feel morally superior to anyone who got involved in this kind of thing, but as a U.S. citizen who moved to Mexico in large part so that my money would instantly be worth a whole lot more—so that I could jump a few social classes without having to put in the work—how could I sit here and judge Mateo? He was trying to take care of his family. He was trying to provide them with a level of comfort and financial security no one in his family had ever experienced.

But still—

This was the *one* thing you did *not* do. Anything else, anything at all. Just not this. Not anywhere, but especially not in Mexico.

And now he wanted out.

But here's the thing: you can't just leave these guys. You can't put in your two weeks' notice and ask your supervisor to serve as a reference. And for what? What's the best case? Go get a job at some construction site and take a 90% pay cut?

"I don't know what to do," he said, looking over at me with eyes way too bright and hopeful, which indicated to me that he was putting far too much faith in a reputation he should have known I didn't deserve.

I'm not a tough guy.

I'm not brave, I'm not courageous.

And I'm certainly not smart. My defining characteristics are indecisiveness and stupidity. My only really desirable trait is that I'm fairly lucky from time to time (but also terribly unlucky at other times).

I wasn't the guy Mateo needed. I didn't know who he did need, or if such a person even existed. I just knew it sure as hell wasn't me.

But I owed this man. I owed him everything. And so I lied to him: "We'll figure something out."

"Chingado, todo esto…"

He was right. Everything *was* fucked.

Out in the water, one of the two Canadians managed to stand up on his board and catch a wave.

He was in this robotic, ninja-like stance, riding straight into shore as opposed to across the face of the wave—but still, he was up on his feet, surfing.

Miracles do happen, I thought, trying my best to convince myself that this was a sign of good things to come, that maybe I really could figure out a way to help Mateo. But this moment of optimism was brief, because just a moment later the Canadian wiped out in fairly ridiculous fashion, the board flying out from underneath him, rocketing up into the air. It looked like the board was about to land on the guy's head, but it ended up missing him by a few inches. At least now I wouldn't have to swim out and try to save the unconscious idiot from drowning (although maybe a water rescue would've been a good thing, because god knows I could've used a karma boost).

Bright sides, Tony. Focus on the bright sides. Like these two: Mateo was only transporting the stuff, and there weren't any border crossings involved. He wasn't growing or manufacturing anything.

As I watched the Canadian resurface and struggle back onto his board, I wondered whether it was a good or bad thing that I'd watched every season of *Narcos,* as well as about a thousand other shows involving drugs in Central America. Good preparation or unnecessary anxiety?

"You ever seen *Narcos*?"

"*¿Qué es eso?*"

"A show on Netflix."

"*¿Qué?*"

"Never mind," I said, and then after a pause: "So where are you getting the stuff? What's the set-up like?"

He looked away, squinting out over the water. I'd never understand why so many Mexicans never wore sunglasses. (I know: I'm a spoiled, wimpy gringo. But still. Christ.)

"I probably need to know a few basic things," I said. "If I'm to be of any help."

"*Está bien,*" he said, and then he told me.

"Come again?"

"Carlos Reyes, out at his farm," he said. "*Lo conoces.*"

I knew him, all right. Carlo Reyes was the farmer who'd taken it upon himself to give a proper burial to one of my victims. Had he not done so, I probably would've been in that 9'x6' cell. Despite a bad habit of covering up homicides committed by expats, Carlos was a solid dude, the kind of guy you'd trust around your wife, kids, money—anything. Which naturally led me to wonder: how in the hell had *he* gotten involved in all this? It didn't make any sense, but given how my life had been unfolding recently, not making sense actually made sense. (If that makes sense?)

What a morning.

What a beautiful fucking morning.

The two people to whom I owed my freedom—Mateo and Carlos—were both now involved in drug trafficking, and at least one of them wanted my help getting themselves out of that situation.

"What's Carlos's opinion on all this? About you wanting out?"

"That it's not a great idea."

"Why's he think that?"

"Because it's not."

I sighed. "Jesus Christ..."

"Jesús Cristo," Mateo echoed in Spanish, a pronunciation I never found to be nearly as cathartic. You need the hard J at the beginning, and then the T at the end gives it a strong, satisfying finish.

I stared down at the sand, thinking about how funny it was—in a tragicomedy sort of way—that things could change so much over the course of a brief conversation. A few words, a couple of minutes, and *bam!*: your life, man, it's fucked.

AUTHOR'S NOTE(S)

(1) This is a work of fiction. While I have never lived in Mexico, my time spent there has always been enjoyable, and not once have I experienced the type of corruption or incompetence described here; Mexicans have been nothing but kind and generous towards me. That said, the country's struggle with corruption has been documented extensively in newspaper articles and investigative reports throughout the years. I have taken creative liberties and adapted these stories for narrative purposes. Should anyone take offense to the characters or descriptions in these frivolous pages, please know that none was intended—failures in this regard are due to my own literary shortcomings. Apologies, also, for any rough or unnatural Spanish translations. I tried. Te lo prometo.

(2) If you enjoyed this book, please consider leaving a review on Goodreads, social media, an online store—wherever. As a self-published author with no marketing budget (or plan), this would help me a great deal. So too would sharing the book with friends. Thanks so much for reading.

(3) Get in touch. There's willzubek.com, or you could also just send a note to willzubek@gmail.com. I'm also, regretfully, sometimes on Twitter and Instagram @willzubek. I'm not sure why.

Made in the USA
Middletown, DE
22 June 2023